Endorsements

Christine Farenhorst once again impresses with her historical research, beautiful stories, and interesting characters. The tales quickly engage, taking you into the European and British world at the time of the 1500 and 1600s. The reader will not quickly forget the intriguing people and the issues of life that are presented. Christians are compelled to think about what living for Jesus in this world is all about. The stories also force us the reader to deal with the tough questions of why a good God allows some terrible things to happen in this world and yet come to see that He is a great and compassionate God. I would highly recommend this volume.

Rev. Al Bezuyen
Covenant Reformed Church
Toronto, Ontario, Canada

Christine Farenhorst brings her characteristically honest, well-researched craft to the five novellas of this book. Set in the often-harsh realities of plague, famine, and persecution of the 16th and 17th centuries, these stories share one central theme: the "strange and wonderful" providence of God. The wonder of God's grace and all-encompassing providence shines out the more brightly against the dark backdrop of man's brokenness and despair. Read and be challenged, moved, and strengthened.

- Cliff and Henrietta Van Dyken

History, sound theology and crackerjack storytelling come wonderfully together in Christine Farenhorst's newest book, The Corner of His Garment. *Five different stories unfold dramatically and yet beautifully communicate the same message of the love of God for His people. Perfect to curl up with on a rainy afternoon when you might desire to get lost in gripping tales from the past while also getting encouraged in the historic Christian faith!*

- Pastor Greg and Charity Bylsma,
Living Water URC, Brantford, Ontario

The Bible comes to us as a story and is filled with stories of God's dealings with His people. In a variety of ways, (historical narrative, poetry, allegory, etc.), God communicates to us in an evocative way. Christians are a people who love stories because our God has revealed Himself to us in that way. Christine Farenhorst has demonstrated herself to be a master storyteller in her past books. Here she has done it again. Readers will once more be regaled with a feast of 'soul full' stories in her unique style. Take, read, and rejoice in the Lamb!

-Rev. Paul Murphy, Pastor
Messiah Reformed Fellowship Church,
Manhattan, New York

The Corner of His Garment

The Corner of His Garment

Stories of the Soul
and the Lamb

Christine Farenhorst

The Corner of His Garment:
Stories of the Soul and the Lamb

Published by Providence Books & Press
Box 3, Site 15, RR2 Barrhead, Alberta, T7N 1N3
www.providencebookspress.com

Printed in USA.

Cover images by Keturah Wilkinson.

ISBN: 978-1-7382729-9-0

Library and Archives Canada Cataloguing in Publication

Title: The corner of his garment : stories of the soul and the lamb /
Christine Farenhorst.
Other titles: Corner of his garment (Compilation)
Names: Farenhorst, Christine, 1948- author.
Description: Second revised edition.
Identifiers: Canadiana 20250204983 | ISBN 9781738272990 (softcover)
Subjects: LCGFT: Short stories. | LCGFT: Christian fiction. | LCGFT:
Historical fiction.
Classification: LCC PS8561.A68 C67 2025 | DDC C813/.54—dc23

Table of Contents

Dedication

to

Gail Wilkinson

Matthew 14:35-36 imparts to us the good news about sick people touching the hem of Jesus garment. The verses read:

And when they had crossed over, they came to land at Gennesaret. And when the men of that place recognized Him, they sent around to all that region and brought to Him all who were sick and implored Him that they might only touch the fringe of His garment. And as many as touched it were made well.

We live in a broken world and as broken people we need answers. Now brokenness does not lie in recognizing cancer, influenza or diabetes; nor does it encompass the feeling of helplessness in the face of these illnesses and other problems. No, the brokenness of humankind lies in the fact that its illnesses and problems are the result of sin.

No matter whom we are in this broken world, we need to recognize two things. The first is that we are spiritually ill, dead actually, and totally helpless in ourselves; and the second is that we need to realize that healing is solely dependent on the power of God.

Gail Wilkinson was a friend, although only for a short while, whom I hope to meet again in heaven. An internationally-acclaimed artist with incredible talent in porcelain, oil, and watercolor, she passed away December 1, 2005. Teaching workshops throughout the United States, Canada, and Europe for over twenty-five years, she won many prestigious awards, illustrated books, and was published in leading art magazines. I had the privilege of first meeting her at my daughter's wedding in 1996 when Gail became my daughter's mother-in-law. A lovely, kind and sharing lady, we got on well together, later becoming grandmothers with a common denominator of six little Wilkinsons.

Brought up as a Jehovah's Witness, Gail had a basic knowledge of Scripture. Leaving that sect in her thirties, she began to dabble in both New Thought and Science of Mind. She liked the emphasis these heresies laid on world peace and the oneness of mankind. However, the peace of heart and mind which she truly sought, eluded her - eluded her until her deathbed. Intensely hungry for that peace as she lay dying, it was the story of the thief on the cross, the thief hanging next to Jesus, which became the fringe of the garment which touched her, covered her and which she held onto.

Consequently, this book is dedicated to her - the epitome of a dead sinner saved by grace - covered by the corner of God's garment.

Foreword

Book forewords are personal, a brief note of acknowledgement between the author, and the one to whom the book is being dedicated. It's a tiny morsel, not even enough to be called an appetizer to the main course. Most forewords are short and are read at a glance as one flips through the pages to the meat in the menu.

I write this because author Christine Farenhorst has a way of making even a book dedication a lump-in-the-throat experience. Perhaps it's because everything she writes is with her eyes focused heavenward. And that disposition changes everything.

Christine has written many short stories over the years. Readers of *Christian Renewal* magazine have come to expect a new short story each Christmas. Some of these find their way into her books. In this volume of five stories, the historical timeline is approximately the same – around the time of the Reformation of the Church in the early 1500s.

Two of the stories are based in Strasbourg, a city on the borders of France and Germany, where Reformed ideas were in collision with the stronghold that dominated life from politics to culture – the teachings of the Roman Catholic Church. Two of the stories are based in England and the Reformation ideas percolating west of the North Sea. To set the stage Christine engages in some name dropping. William Tyndale, Martin Bucer, Oliver Cromwell, King Henry the

Eighth are mentioned in passing providing context to the reader and serving as anchors and markers to this historical fiction.

Many of the terms employed in Christine's stories will also be new to today's reader, but familiar in the 16th century, words such as beguinage, triers, glebe and halberds, to name a few head scratchers – but they are referenced and explained in a glossary at the of the book.

Readers will be introduced to a young orphan boy named Sebastian, an unbeliever named Johann, a girl named Lena, a man named Thomas and his son Tom Drurie, and finally, to David Baxter. Startling in two of the stories is the context of the Plague and its severity which devastated London and parts of Europe during this timeline along with a massive fire alluded to in one of the stories that swept through London following after the Plague.

Christine's descriptive writing, attention to detail and thorough research transport us to an age and time when persecution against those who held to Reformation teachings was real, with life and death consequences. Christians today can thank the Lord for saints who were faithful to the truth even to the point of death.

Thank you, Christine, for inspiring us with these stories, and for helping us to focus our eyes heavenward as well.

John Van Dyk
Editor
Christian Renewal Magazine

Preface

(taken from an excerpt from John Bunyan)

We esteem things according to the price paid for them. The soul has been purchased by a price that the Son and wisdom of God thought appropriate to pay for its redemption. What a thing, then, must be the soul! You must confess that it is of great value. Suppose a prince should descend from his throne, to pick up and put in his bosom, something that he had seen lying trampled under the feet of men. Do you think that he would do this for an old horseshoe, or a trivial thing such as a pin or broken shoelace? Would you not conclude that the thing for which that prince should make such an effort must be a thing of very great worth? Why, this is the case with Christ and the soul! Christ is the Prince, and, as he sat there on the throne of heaven, He looked at the souls of men trampled under the foot of the law and under the penalty of death. What did he do? He came down from His throne, stooped down to earth, and there He laid down His life and blood for them. Would He have done this for inconsiderable things? No, nor would He for the souls of sinners either, if He had not valued them higher than He valued heaven and earth besides.

When I passed by you again
and saw you,
behold,
you were at the age for love,
and I spread the
CORNER OF MY GARMENT
over you
and covered your nakedness;
I made my vow to you
and entered into a covenant with you,
declared the Lord God,
and you
became mine.

Ezekiel 16:8

The Soul and the Lamb

One precious entity within
The body of this discipline,
God's breath, the gift of soul.
Inferior my body is,
Yet this the strange hypothesis,
I value more the role
Of body's ways and body's plays,
Then this eternal soul.

Ten words of law, there are but ten
Commandments given unto men,
And I can keep not one.
Law tramples into dirt. Each word
Has stamp of hell administered
On all I have begun.
Encrusted with the monolith
Of law, I am undone.

Yet soul was bought - and at what price
My soul was bought - a sacrifice,
God's Son, He pitied me.
He saw my end, so stooped to earth,
Laid down His life, gave second birth,
Wed me to purity.
Once profligate, my married state
Brought me infinity.

- Christine Farenhorst

Sebastian's Birth

Jesus answered him, "Truly, truly, I say to you, unless one is born again he cannot see the kingdom of God" (John 3:3).

He was blessed to be living; he was fortunate to be given daily portions of food; and he should be a most grateful child for having a roof over his head. Sebastian, the child, heard that refrain over and over as he crawled, and later toddled, throughout the corridors of a Dominican monastery. Considering that many infants and children of his time died of poverty, malnutrition and disease before they learned how to crawl and toddle, what the boy heard repeated so often was the plain truth: he was very blessed indeed to be breathing.

Sebastian knew very little of family life as other children knew it. He thought it quite normal that the one who fed him and put him to bed every evening was a monk - a monk wearing a long, hooded garment with wide sleeves. Consequently, the word 'brother' not 'mother' was the first one he lisped. When he was just seven years old, and quite old enough to be trusted with running errands at the market square, he saw a woman by the vendors' stalls one day - a woman with a belly as large as the fat ewe in the monastery barnyard. He was not at all fond of the chores he was often sent to do in the barnyard, but the huge belly intrigued him and he contrived to walk alongside the woman. She smiled at him, for he was an attractive, albeit a thin child, with deep blue eyes.

"What is your name?" she queried.

"Sebastian."

"Well, Sebastian, what are you doing out alone at this busy market? Where is your mother?"

"I have a brother," he answered, not quite certain that she would be satisfied with that answer.

There was an altarpiece in the chapel of the monastery, an altarpiece carved out of linden wood. It depicted a lady with faintly reddish cheeks, glancing modestly down at her wooden gown - a wooden gown which was gilded with gold paint. He thought the lady quite beautiful and often stared at her during Mass. She was Mary, he had been told, Mary the mother of the baby Jesus. And were all mothers carved out of linden wood?

"A brother?" the woman repeated, raising her eyebrows, "and does this brother take care of you?"

"Yes," he answered, although a trifle hesitantly, "he does."

The belly moved a little underneath the green skirt swishing next to him. Sebastian could see the satin fabric bulge as if something was poking a small fist into its folds.

"What's that?" he asked.

"What's what?"

He had stopped, and she as well halted her steps. Sebastian laid his right hand on that part of her belly where he had detected the movement. His left hand carried a sack. The belly moved again.

"That," he said.

Studying the child's earnest expression, his wide, blue eyes expectantly searching her own, the woman's face softened into a smile.

"That's my baby," she replied, "and he's telling me he's getting ready to meet his mother soon."

"His mother?"

"Yes," the woman continued to smile down at Sebastian, "his mother, me, the one who has been carrying him about for almost eight months now, even as all mothers carry their children before they are born."

Sebastian's mind puzzled over this reply but only for an instant.

"I have no mother," he countered.

"For certain you did at some point, child," she answered, "all children have a mother at the beginning of their lives."

"But I have never met a mother where I am," Sebastian replied, "except for the statue in the chapel, the statue of Mary. This is a mother. But she has no large belly, nor could she have because she is made of wood."

He stopped, confused by his own speech. The woman hid an upcoming surge of laughter behind her hand.

"You had better not let a priest hear you say things like that," she advised, before she turned and began walking towards a stall that was selling dried herbs.

Sebastian did not follow the woman, but stood gazing after her retreating, bulky figure, thinking on what she had said. A moment later he was forced to turn sideways as a flock of sheep, herded by a peasant shepherd, flooded the pathway between the market stalls where he stood. Protectively grasping the sack holding his purchase of stockfish, Sebastian tried to make himself sturdy, like a tree with deep roots. The sheep were a tad shorter than he was and he remembered with great clarity that dropping and losing something he had been sent to buy for the monastery could cause severe punishment. Yet in spite of his precaution of holding on tightly to the bag of fish, or perhaps because of it, he slipped as two members of the herd, blindly following their shepherd with constant bleating, knocked him down. The dried cod, cod Sebastian had specifically been sent to buy for Brother Sigismund, flew out of the bag as the boy slid onto the mud-packed earth. They landed, neatly spread out, in a pile of horse manure. Brittle, two of the fish broke in half. The sheep kept passing him, a steady stream of wool, bulging eyes fixed on the shepherd as they went. Sebastian picked himself up, gingerly collecting the yellowish, straight pieces of fish. Unsalted, they had been air-dried on wooden racks by Norwegian fishermen who regularly sold them to local Strasbourg merchants. Stockfish were an especial favorite dish of Brother Sigismund who had expressed a wish that morning to have the monastery cook prepare it as stew for his evening meal. The fish, which had already smelled disgustingly strong, now had the added aroma of horse manure cling to it. Sebastian looked around for a place where he might wipe his purchase. One of the nearby stalls had some bales of hay stacked up and he managed to edge close to these bales. Quietly pulling out a handful of the hay, he surreptitiously began to wipe the fish clean.

"Hey, boy, what do you think you're you doing?"

Quickly tucking both hay and the fish into the bag, Sebastian hung his head. But there was no use pretending that he had not heard the question. The voice had been commanding and loud, so loud that a number of passersby turned to look. The owner of the trumpet voice was not long in confronting Sebastian. He was a stout, peasant farmer - a farmer with red hair - and a farmer who possessed a pair of hands like bony pork hocks. The hands reminded Sebastian of Brother Sigismund's hands. Tongue-tied, the child stared up at the man even as he tightly clung to the bag. But as fear threatened to envelop him, a voice came to his aid.

"He did not do anything wrong, Barnabas. Come, Sebastian, I've been looking for you."

It was the woman with the large belly. She had come back from the herb stall and spoke even as she took her place next to him.

"Well," she asked the farmer, "have you never before seen a child who wanted to play with some hay? He's done you no harm, has he? Come along, Sebastian."

The farmer grinned, anger fading from his face.

"If you say so, then it must be true, Frau Kruger."

Still speechless the child found himself unable to move. He clasped the fish bag against his stomach, smelly and hard, the scaly fins digging into his tender skin through the jerkin he wore. The woman put a guiding hand on his neck.

"Come, Sebastian. We're going home."

Automatically he walked alongside his protector. Her hand was gentle but firm and it did not leave his scruff as she guided him through and between the aisles of the myriad sellers towards a quiet spot on the outskirts of the market.

"So," she said, coming to a halt by a well, "I take it you want to wash that fish?"

He nodded, ashamed that he had been so foolish as to fall down and drop the fish and that she had seen this.

"Here is something that might help you with the washing," she went on, pointing to the well, "but you better be quick about it or that brother of yours might skin you instead of the fish."

Then she walked on, turning once to wave at him.

After he had cleaned the fish, Sebastian ran back from the Horse Market to the monastery as fast as his feet could carry him. He crossed the bridge over the canal east of the market - the canal with water flowing through it from the river Ill - and then turned right shortly afterwards onto the lane that led to the Dominican Monastery. In the bag the stockfish, seemingly none the worse for their jaunt, were slightly damp but still rigidly wooden. Cook would have to soak and boil them for several hours, Sebastian knew, to soften them for Brother Sigismund's evening meal. There had been a time two weeks ago when he had dropped a pasty he had been sent to fetch. He had not been able to clean that error off with well water. He could still hear the swish of the birch rod that had been applied to his bottom and he still carried the welts from that beating. Other old scars as well, helped him remember that obedience was a priority. He wished with all his heart that he had a mother - a mother just like the woman who had just helped him. But if what she said was true, then perhaps there was a mother somewhere who belonged to him and he to her.

That evening, before brother Sigismund sent him to his pallet in a small sideroom off the sanctuary, he mustered up enough courage to ask the question he had been mulling over all afternoon.

"Who is my mother, brother Sigismund?"

"Who told you to ask me that?"

Brother Sigismund's voice was metallic and terse. It was not a good sign. Brother Sigismund, tall even when he was sitting, stood up from the high-backed chair in which he had been reclining, his white tunic seemingly trembling with indignation. Sebastian did not understand that indignation and was in awe of it, but he persisted. He was determined to find out what he wanted to know, even if it should cause a dreaded beating.

"No one told me. I just thought of it myself."

"Well think about going to bed."

"But do I not have a mother as all children...."

"Did I tell you to go to bed?"

"Yes."

Sebastian's voice was small. He knew he had lost and that Brother Sigismund would not tell him what he wanted to know. Brother Sigismund had many things on his side: these things included age, size, the prior's confidence, a bad temper, large hands and a birch switch. In view of all these things, Sebastian hung his head and turned to walk towards the door. Opening it, he turned right. His cubicle was just down the hall but in his distress he forgot to close the door behind him.

"And you are not to ask me again. Do you understand that?"

The voice followed him through the open doorway, followed him like a cold breeze. It followed him even as the many rules of the monastery followed him each day. There was the fasting in Advent and Lent, the no eating of meat on Mondays, Wednesdays, Fridays and Saturdays, the 'Our Fathers' recited at the canonical hours and the vigils and prayers offered for the dead; then there were the eternal errands and chores; and there was never any time to play. Indeed, there were so many rules, so many 'you may do this and you may not do that', that Sebastian was convinced that Brother Sigismund must sit down and invent them every evening just so that he could present a new one each day.

After he had washed his face in the bowl of water by his bedside, Sebastian took off his jerkin. Shivering in the thin shift that clung to his skinny torso, he crossed himself and knelt down by his cot. As he knelt, a shadow fell over him. He felt the shadow, although he could not determine whose it was as his eyes were shut and set to pray, and once they were shut they ought not to open.

"Your mother," it was Brother Sigismund's shadow who spoke slowly and deliberately, "was a Jewess - a Jewess from Regensburg."

Sebastian now opened his eyes. This was a new word.

"A Jewess?" he repeated, "What is a Jewess?"

"Never mind," Brother Sigismund said, and again, "Never mind. It is enough that you should know she was one. Now finish your prayers and go to sleep."

Sent to help Brother Klaus, the cook, the following afternoon, Sebastian tried to work up the courage to ask what had been niggling on his mind all morning. Sitting on a stool, peeling onions, alternately wiping the tears that formed in his eyes and pulling off the thin layers of the vegetables, his usual chatter was not forthcoming.

"What ails you," Brother Klaus eventually asked, flaccid jowls shaking as he spoke, "Did a rat eat away part of your tongue last night, so that you cannot be part of some conversation. Come, Sebastian, at least sing me a song if you will not speak."

Now Sebastian loved to sing. But it was not a song that spilled out of his mouth but the question that had been planted there by Brother Sigismund.

"What is a Jewess?" he asked and he asked the question quietly and yet so succinctly that the words rang clear to the rafters.

"A Jewess?" Brother Klaus disbelievingly repeated, turning his rotund body around from his task of plucking a chicken to stare at the child, while he reiterated, "A Jewess?"

"Yes," Sebastian affirmed, nodding his head without looking up from the pile of onions, "for this is what Brother Sigismund said my mother was."

"Oh," cook replied, turning back to the chicken.

"Brother Sigismunch said ... that is, I think he meant, that this was something very bad."

"Yes," cook agreed, bowing his head over the fowl in his hands, "I do believe it is thought so by many."

"Why?"

"I think it is probably true that being a Jewess is something evil," cook spoke slowly, continuing to pluck feathers, "but it is a kind of evil that I cannot explain to you. You are too young."

"But I must know," the boy insisted, "for I did not even know that I had a mother of my own until yesterday. And I am growing older every day."

"I think," answered cook, inspired by a sudden thought, "that it would be better for us to talk about ... about your name. You know that your name is Sebastian, don't you?"

"Yes," Sebastian answered.

"Well, do you know why your name is Sebastian?"

"No," the boy's answer came grudgingly, for he knew that his original question was being sidestepped and it irked him that it would not be answered.

"It is because you came here to the monastery on January 20 in the year of our Lord 1521. January 20 is the feast day of St. Sebastian, that Christian martyr who ..."

"But _how_ did I come here?"

"I do not know that," Brother Klaus replied, rather irritated, not looking up from the chicken which he had finished plucking and was now washing in a basin, "you were just here one day and I was not privy as to the how of it."

"Did I come wrapped up in a mother's belly?"

Brother Klaus wearily waved his hands in the air before he asked, "Have you quite finished with the onions? I need them now to stuff this bird's belly."

Sebastian got up and brought the onions to him in a wooden dish.

"Here."

"And," cook went on, "now find me the parsley, some ginger, pepper, cinnamon and salt. I'm going to show you how to mix these things together with some swine suet, boil them and then stuff them into the chicken."

Sebastian did as he was asked and then watched Brother Klaus in silence as he prepared the bird. There was no more talk about babies or where he came from or how he came to be in the monastery. When the bird was finally roasting over the spit Brother Klaus clapped his hand hard on Sebastian's shoulder.

"We'll make a fine cook out of you yet, boy."

"I do not want to be a cook," Sebastian stubbornly replied staring down at the floor, "I want to be someone's son."

"Ah," said Brother Klaus and then stopped, because he did not know what else he ought to say and because, in spite of himself, he was rather fond of the boy.

The city of Strasbourg where the monastery stood, lay on a plain, just below where the river Ill met the river Breusch before it ran down to the Rhine. Its skyline was dominated by church spires. But the church spire of Strasbourg's grand Cathedral was higher than any of the other buildings in the city. Although the Cathedral's two towers were high, this single spire was known to be the tallest in all of Europe. Also, the huge, rose-colored stained-glass window between the two towers had become a landmark of great importance to many visitors. Strasbourg, often referred to as the metropolis of the upper Rhine, encompassed some six hundred and twenty acres - acres which were home to about twenty thousand people. The walls enclosing the city held ten pedestrian gates as well as a massive water gate through which both the Ill and Breusch flowed majestically into the city's numerous canals. Strasbourg boasted many religious houses. There was, of course, the Dominican monastery which Sebastian called home. But there were also eight other religious orders, nine women's convents, and several dozen chapels. Almost all of the orders and convents had been shut down by the town council, the reason being that most of the men on the town council were of the new evangelical sort. One might possibly conclude that the people of Strasbourg were godly-minded. That, however, was for God to judge. But there was no denying that Strasbourg lived and breathed trade. Her ports both collected and exported wine and grain from both sides of the Upper Rhine. There was business in meat, salt, oil, sheets, metals, fish and fur. The canals transported many goods. The book industry was booming and fishermen, butchers, metal-workers, goldsmiths, tinsmiths, coopers, furriers and painters all mixed and interacted in the busy, pulsating, day to day heartbeat of the inner city.

Yet the truth was that an air of unrest was positioned over Strasbourg and the surrounding countryside. The recent Peasant Revolt was still fresh on everyone's mind. There was general discontent about the rising cost of loans coupled with a series of mediocre harvests. The clergy were fat and the greater part of the population of the city was lean. Beggars abounded in the streets and food prices had risen. Although the city itself had opened its granaries to the destitute, it was noted that the church was unwilling to open her doors to help the poor. Was it because the priests were more concerned about their stomachs than the poor people in their care? Was it because the church held the poor to be heretics - heretics being those people who leaned towards the new teaching of the man Martin Luther? These things were spoken of in taverns, in market places and in homes everywhere. And the truth was that these 'heretics' now outnumbered the Catholics and no one could argue the figures.

Mid-afternoon, a few weeks after his first encounter with the woman at the market, Sebastian saw her again. Sent on another errand, he stood very still for a moment when he spotted her. Hesitant about approaching, as he painfully recalled their previous encounter, he only observed her from a distance. Once more a customer at the herb booth, she was concentrating on the wares. He noted that her face seemed thinner whereas the rest of her body had grown. As he studied her, she appeared to him to be so weary that he summoned up all his courage and moved closer, shyly offering to carry her basket when she turned around to move on.

"Why, young Master Sebastian," she exclaimed, and her face broke into a smile, even as her eyes searched his frame, studying him very carefully, "and have you bought some more fish today?"

He shook his head, even as he put out his hand to take her basket. She permitted him to do so.

"You are a good boy," she praised, as he dangled the basket from his right arm, "and that is the truth of it. Well then, if you are not buying fish, you must tell me what you are about today."

"I had to deliver a mmm... message for Brother Sigismund," he stuttered, hating himself for it, for he did want to make a good impression.

"And have you delivered it?" she questioned.

He nodded, still swinging the wood woven basket.

"Good," she replied, "then I would be most pleased if you would escort me home."

From being heavy his heart grew light and glad, for he wished for some inexplicable reason to stay close to her. Together they passed the bridge over the river Ill, even as he always did when he went home. But where he was wont to turn right onto the lane that led to the Dominican Monastery, they walked straight on.

"I do not know your name," he suddenly blurted out as they reached the corner of the Judengasse, the Jews' Street, where a number of great and fashionable families lived. Perhaps because it was named Jews' Street, he suddenly thought that this might be the place where his mother lived.

"It is Frau Kruger."

"Oh," he answered as he swung the basket hard, now remembering that this was what the red-headed farmer had called her.

She stopped for a moment, leaning against a stone wall at her right, breathing irregularly.

"Are you all right?"

"Yes, I am just a little weak. The babe is kicking hard."

He did not know what to do or to say and stood quietly at her side.

"Can I lean on you, little Sebastian? A great, big woman like myself?"

She smiled as she spoke but it was a weak smile and he straightened his shoulders, making himself stretch tall.

"Yes."

She put her left hand on his right shoulder and he felt the weight of her threaten to push him down. But he did not buckle and walked slowly and carefully forward along the road. They proceeded in this way for almost ten minutes without speaking and then she halted - halted in front of a half-timbered house. Its timber was painted black, even as all the houses on the street had their timber painted black. The walls between the timber were all of a lighter color and each home had a peaked roof ornamented with gables. There were a few steps leading up to the front door. Frau Kruger let go of Sebastian's shoulder and began her ascent up the steps. He followed behind, thinking that he would catch her should she trip or fall. But she seemed to have received an increase in energy for she made it to the top without any problem. Reaching the door, she turned.

"Well, my fine protector," she asked, "Will you come in and sit with me for a while?"

For a split-second Sebastian thought of Brother Sigismund and the punishment which would surely be meted out to him for not returning to the monastery directly. But when he gazed up at Frau Kruger's kind face, he capitulated to the temptation of the pleasure of being with someone who was so intensely sweet and beautiful.

"Yes," he answered briefly, "I will."

Frau Kruger's eyes crinkled with pleasure as she smiled. Her hand lifted to knock on the great oaken frame of the door. It was opened moments later by tall woman. Wearing a dark blue dress and a white cap, she immediately ushered Frau Kruger inside with an air of genuine care and concern.

"This is Sebastian," Frau Kruger said by way of introduction as they walked in, "and he is to visit with me and have a cup of cider, Anna. Will you bring it to us in my sitting room upstairs?"

Sebastian followed Frau Kruger and Anna through a tiled foyer up a long, winding stairs. He did not have to worry about Frau Kruger stumbling on her way up, as Anna had put her arm protectively around her mistress' waist. The stairs were made of wood, polished wood, and the steps felt smooth underneath his shoes - shoes made of stiff pieces of leather, stitched together and tied at the ankle. They had been made by the monastery shoemaker and they creased as his feet carried him up. At the top of the stairs, there was a landing. A portrait of a man and a woman hung on the wall of the landing. They were a well-dressed pair. The woman stood in front. She was dark-haired and wore a small cream-colored cap which perched prettily on the back of her head. A white fichu encompassed her neck. Her dress was blue - not like Anna's blue dress but a lighter blue. The man wore a dark jacket and stood behind her. His left hand rested lovingly on her shoulder the way, Sebastian reflected, that Frau Kruger's hand had rested on his shoulder. The eyes of the man were friendly, but the woman, although her eyes were wide open, had a strange look in them. The portrait fascinated Sebastian as he mounted the steps towards it. At the top of the stairs he paused a long moment in front of it, both intrigued and drawn. To his right Anna opened a door. It creaked and brought Sebastian back to where he was. Turning away from the picture, he followed the women. They walked through the wide-open door side by side. Anna deposited her mistress onto a low chair in the center of the room. Breathing hard with the effort of climbing, Frau Kruger closed her eyes. Uncertain as to what to do, Sebastian stood in the doorway. But then she opened her eyes.

"Well, young man," she invited, "Come in and sit by me."

Anna walked out past him, stroking him kindly on the head as she did so. Rich, elaborate tapestries hung on the walls, lending warmth and coziness to the room. Fenestral windows, with lattice frames covered in a fabric soaked in resin and tallow, let through the sunlight. He stared at these windows, for he had never seen such windows before. At the monastery they had glass windows.

"Will they do?"

She closed her eyes again as she spoke and the boy noted once more just how pale she was. There was another chair by her side. She patted it and, almost on tiptoes, he approached.

"Are you sure you do not want to go to sleep," he whispered.

"No, I do not want to sleep."

Her eyes were open wide now and she winked at him, before she continued.

"But I do want to hear all about you, young man, and how it happens to be that you are living in the Dominican monastery."

He replied by saying what had been uppermost on his mind these last few weeks.

"My mother was a Jew."

She was silent and regarded him intently before she responded.

"And that is why you are in the monastery?"

"I do not know," he answered truthfully, "no one will tell me anything of it. I have been asking but ...."

"Well," she said softly when he stopped speaking, "I know what it is like to live within the walls of a place. That is to say, I used to live in a convent - in a Dominican convent, actually. It was St. Margaret's here in Strasbourg."

"You did?"

Sebastian knew what a convent was and he knew where St. Margaret's convent was. Father Lebentorff, who had been the father confessor of St. Margaret's, had visited Brother Sigismund a number of times and he had brought the two of them cider.

"Yes," Frau Kruger nodded from her place in the chair, "and would you like me to tell you how I came to be in the convent?"

"Yes, please."

"I was but a child of some eight years of age, perhaps close to your age," she began, "and I lived with an aunt in Nuremburg. My parents died when I was seven. First my father died and shortly afterwards my mother. My aunt, who was my mother's sister, and who had stood godmother to me when I was baptized, took me into her home. But," and here she paused for a moment, "my aunt had six children of her own and I seemed to be in the way. So she arranged for the convent to take me in."

"But," Sebastian interposed, "you are here now. Did the nuns in the convent allow you to leave?"

Anna re-entered the room quietly, carrying two cups of cider. She set them down on a low table at her mistress' side and before leaving, bent over to adjust the pillow in Frau Kruger's back.

"Are you comfortable?" she asked, "Are you sure you do not want to go up to bed for a rest?"

"No, Anna, my dear help," Frau Kruger answered, "I am quite comfortable here and am about to tell Sebastian here about my convent days. Do you want to stay and hear the story again?"

Anna straightened her body and sniffed in a disdainful sort of way.

"No, I do not, but," and here she fixed her eyes on Sebastian, "make sure you come for me should Frau Kruger have any need."

Sebastian nodded fervently. Of course, he would do that. Satisfied, Anna left the room.

It was quiet for a long moment. Then Frau Kruger took up her tale once more.

"I had no consciousness of any vocation at the time my aunt told me I was to go and live with nuns. As a matter of fact, I had no desire at all to enter a convent. But she gave me no choice."

Her voice had turned monotone. Sebastian, looking directly at her face, had the distinct impression that she did not even know that he was still there.

"There were those in the nunnery who did desire to be there. There was one girl, seven years of age, a year younger than I was, who was full of zeal to become a nun. She was a cripple and limped. She told me none would love her save Jesus because of her infirmities. There is a rhyme, Sebastian," Frau Kruger went on in a manner a bit more lively, now looking straight at the boy, "and it goes thus:

Now earth to earth in convent walls,
To earth in churchyard sod.
I was not good enough for man,
And so am given to God."

Frau Kruger stopped for a moment after she had recited the verse, and repeated the last line slowly.

"And so am given to God ... and actually that was the truth of it. Yes, that was the truth of it. I did not know it at the time, but there is only one Hand that writes each day."

Sebastian tried hard to follow Frau Kruger, but his face registered incomprehension. Frau Kruger saw it and went on trying to explain.

"There was a deaf and dumb girl as well in the convent. She was given to God also. You see there were always relatives who desired to get rid of children so they might get their hands on an inheritance. I also had a small inheritance of some four hundred guilders. At least I believe it was four hundred guilders, but it disappeared within the belly of the convent."

Frau Kruger stopped, bent over to reach for her cup of cider and brought it to her lips. Sebastian reached likewise. It was not often that he was given well-spiced cider in the monastery and he savored its taste.

"Did your aunt want to get rid of you?" Sebastian ventured, even as his hands embraced the warmth of the cup.

"My aunt ...," Frau Kruger thoughtfully murmured, "Yes, I suppose that she did in a way. But never mind, for she has since died and her husband has remarried. I should speak no ill of the dead and perhaps my aunt sincerely worried that she would not be able to ... to care for me properly ... to give me enough attention. But I did not mean to speak of that. I only meant to tell you how I came to be in the convent and then how I came to leave the convent."

She slowly took another sip of her hot cider before she continued. Sebastian noticed that the babe within her was lively, kicking the folds of her garment with gusto, and he wondered greatly at the mystery of a baby within a woman. Had he so kicked his mother?

"I now want to tell you of the man who was sent to the convent just a few years ago. We did have our own chaplain, a father confessor, but he was dismissed by the council of Strasbourg when the new faith became stronger in the city."

"The new faith?" questioned Sebastian.

"Yes, child," Frau Kruger said, "the new faith. And have none of the brothers spoken to you of it? I supposed that they might have told you about it in ridicule, might have mocked it and told you to stay away from it."

Sebastian shook his head, "No, I have not heard anyone speak of it."

"Well, I will speak of it to you now."

She stroked her belly as she spoke and leaned back.

"This man who came to our convent, his name was Dr. Martin Bucer. He was appointed by the city council of Strasbourg to preach to us at St. Margaret's thrice a week. Our prioress, Ursula Bock, was very displeased by the council's order. I had no great love for the prioress, for she was strict. Truth be told, she was a sour lady, and she bore me no love. But I did not strive to have love or understanding of her situation and that was perhaps wrong of me ...."

Here Frau Kruger paused for a while before she went on. Sebastian contemplated that Frau Bock, the sour prioress, sounded remarkably like Brother Sigismund. Should he perhaps try to have understanding for Brother Sigismund's constantly bad temper? It had never occurred to him.

"The truth of it was," Frau Kruger continued, "that because Ursula Bock was displeased at this man's coming, I was very pleased. The truth of it was that anything that displeased her, pleased me - and vice versa - anything that pleased her, displeased me. Before Dr. Bucer came, the prioress spoke to everyone at the convent. She told us to stop up our ears, to not listen, and to say Hail Mary's in our heart while he was talking. I was one of the younger ones at the convent. I had not taken my vows as yet even though I was pushed strongly to think on it. I think I wished to stave off what seemed to me to be a life prison sentence. I had no desire to be forever enclosed within the walls of the convent."

Frau Kruger sighed audibly and pushed her head hard against the cushions Anna had propped up behind her. Sebastian companionably sighed with her, at the same time admiring the tapestry on the wall behind her chair. It had a tree with apples hanging on it and a brook ran underneath the tree. He had never seen anything as lovely as that tapestry, although perhaps the stained-glass windows at the great Cathedral came close.

"Dr. Bucer was a robust, rather portly man who wore a black robe. His voice was not overly loud but we heard every word he said, we who were assembled before him. He spoke kindly and said he wished us well but then he went on to say things we had never heard before. He told us that the convent was bad not only for our spiritual lives but also for our physical lives. Ursula Bock gasped at this and put her hands over her ears. Many of the nuns followed her example. But I listened."

Sebastian was fascinated by Frau Kruger's words. No one had ever spoken to him in the monastery as she now spoke to him. That was not to say that no one ever spoke to him. But words were usually spoken to him in the form of commands, not in the form of conversation.

"You know, Sebastian," Frau Kruger's voice went on, lilting in a sudden joy, "people accused Dr. Bucer of being the child of a Jewess? It came to my heart just now as you mentioned your mother. Not, mind you, child, that it is wrong to be the child of a Jewess, for was not our blessed Lord Jesus the child of a Jewess?"

Here she smiled such a broad smile at Sebastian that he grinned back. He did not quite understand what her words meant but they nevertheless comforted him.

"In any case, around the third or fourth time that Dr. Bucer came to St. Margaret's to preach, Ursula Bock instructed some of us to stand behind the choir screen so that we would be more or less hidden from his view. She thought that in this way we would be less influenced by what he said. When he did not object to some of the nuns standing behind the screen, she next ordered that some of the angels beside the high altar be dressed in habits and veils, and that they be placed behind the choir screen. When the sermon ended these angels were pulled away and the nuns took their place behind the screen again. She thought in this way to fool Dr. Bucer."

Sebastian laughed.

"Did he find out what the prioress was doing?"

"Not in the beginning. In the beginning he thought that the motionless figures of the angels behind the screen meant that the nuns were very impressed by what he said. But when he found out, and I've forgotten how he found out that he had been tricked, he complained to the city council. The council immediately ordered all the nuns to attend every single one of Dr. Bucer's sermons while sitting in the nave with the lay folk, directly next to the pulpit."

"Did you have to sit next to the pulpit?"

"I never hid behind the choir screen but always sat in the nave. There was not enough room behind the screen for all of us. I loved to listen. Dr. Bucer preached well, Sebastian. He explained the words of Holy Scripture to those who were listening."

"Which words?" Sebastian wanted to know.

"Well, there are many words in Holy Scripture, but the most important words he explained were surely ones that told me that someone is saved through faith in Jesus Christ; that someone is saved simply by being born as a little child into His arms and His care. I had always thought I must work, work and work to maybe be saved. But Dr. Bucer said, over and over, that a person could be saved simply by having faith, by being born again."

"Born like ...?"

Sebastian did not finish his sentence but pointed to his mentor's stomach. She laughed.

"Yes, in a way, I suppose. But being born again means having faith in Jesus; believing in Him and in His love for you. Not trusting in your own works."

"What works did you do?"

Frau Kruger smiled.

"Probably a lot of the same works that you do in the monastery, Sebastian, works that you are ordered to do each day."

"Were you ... were you ever beaten if you did not ... not do them?"

At these words, she sat up straight in her chair and eyed the boy carefully.

"Are you beaten often, Sebastian?"

"Yes," he answered softly, staring past her at the tapestry, seeing, not the tree, but the ever-present birch rod in brother Sigismund's hand - a hand that always had dirty fingernails.

"Do you not work hard at your tasks?"

"Yes," he answered even softer, "and someday I shall run away even as you did."

"So you would like to leave the monastery?"

"Yes, but I have no place to go. I will wait a little while until I am bigger and stronger ... and ...."

He stopped for he had not yet thought the thing through properly. Presently it was just a feeling, a dream that often came on him as he lay sleeping on his cot at night.

"Where did you go," he puzzled on, "after you left the convent?"

"Well, Dr. Bucer continued to teach regularly from the Bible, and then the magistrates of the city came to visit St. Margaret's. They informed all the nuns they need not obey the prioress any longer. They stipulated that Mass would no longer be said, and that choir duties would be abolished. Then they told us that we were free to leave the convent and that even all those nuns who had already taken their vows would be free from these vows if they left, and free from the rules they had promised to obey."

"I wish the magistrates would come to the monastery where I stay," Sebastian longingly mouthed, adding persistently, "But where did you go after you left?"

"I had spoken to Dr. Bucer about my wish to leave and he told me I was welcome to come to his home, that I could stay with him and his wife, Elisabeth."

"But you are not staying with them now."

"No, indeed," Frau Kruger continued, "for while I stayed with them, I met a man who visited their house. A man who has just traveled in from visiting Regensburg. And his name was Philip Kruger."

"Regensburg?" Sebastian repeated wonderingly, and again, "Regensburg? That is where brother Sigismund says my mother came from."

"Yes, indeed," Frau Kruger agreed, looking at him rather strangely, or so he thought, "that is what you have told me."

"Perhaps then," the boy went on wistfully, "perhaps he, this Philip Kruger, knew my mother and if he did, do you suppose he might tell me about her?"

"Yes," Frau Kruger answered instantly, pulling her heavy body out of the chair and standing up as she spoke, "I'm sure that he would. But I think that now, if you have finished your cider, you must go back, for if you are missed unduly ...."

She did not finish her sentence, but Sebastian knew how it would have ended had she finished it. He would be punished. He minded it not at this very minute for it was so very comfortable here. It was almost as if he belonged here. Frau Kruger placed a hand on his head.

"Sebastian," she said softly, "the very best thing that Dr. Bucer told me was that Jesus left heaven to become a child, a boy child like you. He came to earth, to this place where we live, so that He might carry our sins and save us."

"Where is heaven?"

Sebastian stood up also and walked with her to the door as they spoke.

"Have not the monks spoken to you of heaven? Heaven is where God lives. It is beautiful there. There is no pain. There are no tears. Everything is good. Heaven is the home of God."

"Brother Sigismund speaks to me of purgatory and hell," Sebastian answered darkly, "This, he says, is where I will go after I die and I will be there for a long, long time. But he has not spoken of heaven, except that only the very good go there. He says that it is of no use telling me about it because I will probably not go there because I am not very good."

Frau Kruger pushed her right hand into the crook of her back as they walked through the doorway. She moved very slowly.

"And Jesus left heaven?" Sebastian questioned as an afterthought, "I do not understand why He would do so if it was so good."

They paused underneath the portrait of the man and the woman. It seemed now as if the couple were looking directly at Sebastian. But he did not stare back at them. He was too intent upon the answer Frau Kruger was formulating."

"Yes, He left it."

She said no more than that. She did not really have a chance because Sebastian shot back at her words of disbelief.

"If you have a place where there is no pain or crying, why would you leave it? I do not believe that Jesus, or anyone would leave such a beautiful place as you say heaven is, to come here where boys are beaten and where monks can do wicked things."

"Does Brother Sigismund do wicked things, Sebastian?"

They were standing at the top of the stairs now, and the polished wood glimmered with a reddish sort of glow. Sebastian ran his shoe along the edge of the first stair.

"I am all right," the boy spoke softly, "I do not cry," and then he added as an afterthought, "I have seen the figures of Mary and the baby Jesus, but I truly did not know that He was in heaven before He came here and I truly do not understand why he would leave it."

"Well, He came down to earth from heaven because He loved us," Frau Kruger said softly, her eyes bright and tender, and fixed upon Sebastian, "He became a little child, a small baby, just like you were and just like I was. But," she added, even as the baby in her belly noticeably moved, "He had no sin."

She stopped and rubbed the small of her back before she went on, her voice even softer.

"When we believe in Him, the God-Child Who came to die for us, then we, you and I, Sebastian, have been born again ...."

She stopped once more and breathed in deeply. Sebastian was silent. He had heard urgency mingled with love in Frau Kruger's voice and it filled the boy with a desire to understand and believe what she believed. Trying to verbalize his thoughts, he cleared his throat, but looking up saw that her face had suddenly changed into a grimace, a grimace of pain. She took hold of the balustrade.

"I think you must call Anna," she said weakly, "for I believe that the baby is coming, and then you must run back to the monastery, Sebastian. I would not have it that you got into trouble for overstaying. But we will speak again, you and I."

He ran down the stairs, only looking back once over his shoulders to see that Frau Kruger had sat down at the top of the steps, her head leaning against one of the newels. He found Anna in a room which he supposed was the kitchen and she, after noting his troubled face, straightway ran past him to find her mistress. He stood quietly for a moment and wondered if he should leave. But leaving was, after all, what

Frau Kruger had told him to do. His feet traced their way back to the front door. Slowly he opened it and with one more backward glance over his shoulder to the stairs which now lay empty, he stepped outside. Bright sunlight enveloped him. He closed the door behind him with a small thud, sucked in a mouthful of fresh air, and began his journey back.

Brother Sigismund was waiting for him. That is to say, when Sebastian tried to slip quietly into his duties in the kitchen, taking the broom into his hands as soon as his foot crossed the threshold, brother Klaus's voice rang out from where he was standing by the hearth.

"You must go to Brother Sigismund's cell, Sebastian."

"But I have not yet begun to sweep," Sebastian protested, his heart sinking within him, "and I must feed the ...."

"No, you must go at once," Brother Klaus insisted, "for I think he was greatly concerned that you were gone for such a long time."

Slowly Sebastian leaned the broom back against the wall. He was afraid. He knew he had been gone a long time but had hoped against hope on the way home that perhaps his absence had not been noted. Now Brother Sigismund would surely be very angry with him. He lost his temper easily, even over so small a thing as spilling one's food. He recalled that as a very little boy of perhaps two or three summers he had once knocked down a mug of cider and that it had cascaded like a wave over the wooden table in the refectory. A hush had descended amongst all the Dominican brothers at board and then Brother Sigismund had stood up.

"Come with me, Sebastian," he had said, holding out his large hand.

He would never forget that as he had put his chubby fist into that hand, how that hand had squeezed his own very hard. It had squeezed so hard that tears had sprung into his eyes. Brother Sigismund had led him to a cell, a cell reserved for punishment. It was a cell where all too often he had been locked up for wetting his cot, for soiling himself at night when he had been too afraid to rise and find the reredorter. And then he had been whipped. He failed to understand then and now why he should have been whipped so hard. His footsteps slow to begin with, grew slower as they approached Brother Sigismund's room. But even at their snail's pace, they eventually reached the door. He knocked timidly.

"Come in."

Brother Sigismund's voice did not sound angry, or impatient. Perhaps this would simply be a teaching time - a time in which he would learn a new rule as he often did. His hand reached for the door handle, pushing it open.

"Ah, Sebastian, I have been waiting for you."

Sebastian stood in the doorway, uncertain as to whether this was a conciliatory sentence or not.

"Where, might I ask, have you been?"

"I ... I helped a lady walk home ...," he hesitatingly began, stuttering slightly, "She was ... was tired and leaned on me for help. That is why ...."

"What was her name?"

Brother Sigismund's eyes were pressed half-shut. Sebastian began to tremble. There was no warmth in that face. None at all. Should he tell Brother Sigismund Frau Kruger's name? If he did, would he be betraying the friendship that she had given?

"I don't ... don't know," he said after a long pause, feeling ill at ease because, after all, his answer was a lie.

"You walked a woman home and you don't even know her name?"

Sebastian hung his head. He was at a loss.

"She was a nice lady," he whispered to the floor, "a beautiful lady and she was kind to me."

"Nice?! Beautiful?! Kind?!"

Brother Sigismund made the words sound as if they had been dipped in a mud puddle. Sebastian raised his eyes to those of his tormentor.

"Yes, she was," he bravely ventured, "and I am glad I helped her."

"So each time you are sent on an errand, I will not be able to trust you?"

"You can trust me."

Sebastian's voice trembled and he looked away from Brother Sigismund. He loved going out on errands. He loved leaving the four walls of the monastery behind him. He loved seeing the sky, feeling the wind on his face, and hearing people speak as he made small purchases or delivered messages. Would Brother Sigismund now forbid him this?

"You must be punished, Sebastian."

Sebastian nodded. He knew punishment was inevitable and he steeled his body for the rod that would in a moment magically appear in Brother Sigismund's hand.

"From now on you will no longer have your own cell to sleep in. You will sleep with the pigs."

Slowly Sebastian drew his eyes away from where they had been fixed to a crack on the wall behind brother Sigismund, to brother Sigismund's face.

"With ... with the pp ... pigs?" he whispered.

"When you do not come back to the monastery after you have been sent on an errand, it obviously means you do not value the place you have here. Your cubicle will be taken away and you will, from now on, live with the pigs."

Sebastian did not reply but looked down at the floor. Within his mind's eye he could clearly see the small outdoor enclosure where several hogs were raised for the monastery's consumption, hogs who were slaughtered every fall. The fenced off area had a bare mud floor and he had watched the animals root voraciously into the soil. Brother Thomas, who often slopped the hogs, had told him they did so to protect themselves from heat. Sometimes brother Klaus sent Sebastian to feed the pigs table scraps that were left over. He did not care for the task. The smell was overpowering and he was always happy to leave as quickly as possible.

"You know where the straw is kept. You can fetch some and place it alongside the hog pen. This will serve as your bedding."

Sebastian nodded not actually knowing why he did so.

"You will not be beaten this time."

Brother Sigismund's voice was low, very smooth, and when Sebastian cautiously raised his eyes again, he was surprised to see a thin smile hovering on the monk's face. But it was not the same kind of smile that Frau Kruger had given him. This was a smile that smothered and took one's breath away.

"You may leave now. Sleep well, Sebastian. And report to me in the morning after matins."

Sebastian turned, his feet doing his thinking. As he left brother Sigismund's room, they automatically carried him past the sanctuary, through the halls, to the outside door, eventually guiding him to the shed where the bales of straw were kept. It was twilight. As if in a trance, his arms began to gather a few handfuls of the prickly stuff. But he could not bring himself to carry the straw over to the hog pen. Instead he dropped it onto the ground where he was standing. Then he began burrowing into the hayloft itself. He was used to sleeping on a straw pallet, but a tick was sewn around that straw and there was a coverlet overtop to keep him warm. Like a mouse he burrowed now, and in a while found himself encased in new-mown, fresh-smelling straw. It comforted him somewhat, to be surrounded thus by the straw. It embraced him, even though it was a stubbly embrace. He lay quietly and pondered again about how kind Frau Kruger had been. He wondered how she was and if the baby within her had come, although he knew not how this would occur. And then he was filled with a great desire to go back and tell her about what had happened to him here and how he had been told to sleep outside with the pigs. The baby Jesus had slept on straw in a stable. That much he did know. Now he was just like the baby Jesus. Why would Jesus have left the beautiful place of heaven, a place which was probably more beautiful than Frau Kruger's house? Because He loved Sebastian and wanted to carry his sins? It was nice to have someone carry something for you. And the weariness and pain within his belly were heavy - very heavy.

He awoke a few hours later and wondered if it were already time to rise for matins. Quietly extricating himself from the straw he stood next to the hayloft, undecided as to what he should do. If he went in and sat down in the sanctuary, he would be sure not to miss the morning prayers. But he had no desire at all to go back into the monastery. He noted a wooden cart standing next to the hog pen. Suppose he were to crawl into the cart and cover himself with a little straw. It was chilly enough so that he would be sure not to sleep too deeply and while he was lying in the cart he could think about what he ought to do. Or perhaps he would just lie on the wooden slats and gaze up at the stars. Gathering a great many bunches of straw, he carried them over to the cart and tossed them over its wooden edge. Next he climbed into the cart and lay down. The sky above him blinked cheerfully with reassuring light. And Sebastian mouth was strangely moved to sing words from prayers he chanted with the monks:

"God, come to my assistance; Lord make haste to help me."

He had never really thought deeply about these words before, but now, staring up at the stars and shivering underneath the sparse collection of straw, he became conscious of the fact that there was no one else but God; and that he was truly able to ask God for help. He also became aware that his fears slowly began to ebb away, ebb away like water into dry soil. Indeed, his eyelids began to plague him for sleep and he soon succumbed, hands folded on his chest.

When he next woke, it was to the sound of voices. One of the voices he recognized - recognized faintly - the other he did not know.

"Hsst, Peter, or you'll wake all the monks and then there'll be a row."

A snort of laughter followed.

"Be quiet yourself, Barnabas and help me hitch this mule to the cart so that we might be off."

Sebastian, who was curled up under the straw against the front side of the cart, eased himself up and peeped over the edge. Dimly he saw the outlines of two men busily fitting a rope halter over the head of a donkey.

"Hold the beast still!" the voice that Sebastian did not know spoke again, "or we shall never be on our way."

"Hold him still yourself," the one called Barnabas replied, "one donkey should know another."

More laughter followed. Sebastian was at a loss as to what to do and stayed very quiet. At length both men turned, having finished fitting the mule, and proceeded to climb up onto the driver's seat. The boy ducked down again, covering himself best he could with the straw. His heart was pounding.

"Well, where are we to pick up the boy?" the one called Peter asked.

"We've already picked him up," Barnabas replied, "He's asleep in the wagon behind us. I've been watching him most of the evening and I think the child is tuckered out."

Sebastian rolled towards the center of the wagon. He did not understand the gist of the conversation, but knew that it involved himself. As soon as he was able, he would climb out of the wagon and run, where to he knew not, but surely, he ought not to stay here.

"Why does he want this child ...?"

Peter let the question dangle in the air and Sebastian did not know who 'he' was, nor what it was 'he' wanted done. But the answer enlightened him.

"Brother Sigismund wants the child's money for the monastery and, I dare say, some batzen will line his own pocket as well."

"How...?" Peter began again.

"It is the child's inheritance he is after. We are supposed to dispose of the boy somewhere, somewhere neatly out of the monastery's way."

The wagon had begun to hobble forward and Sebastian durst not move for fear of being found out.

"It's a beautiful night," remarked the voice that was Peter.

"Morning more like," said Barnabas, "and the gates of the city should be open by now I would think. Ah, and here is our friend, Brother Sigismund, to speed us on I think.

Out of the shadows a hooded figure approached the wagon. Barnabas clucked and the donkey, braying softly, halted.

"You have the child? Has he been suffocated?"

Sebastian was now gripped by a coldness that seemed to turn him into stone. He had not cared for Brother Sigismund, had never fooled himself into thinking that the monk was fond of him, but he had not in a thousand years supposed that the man would be so callous as to actually want him dead. His whole body froze and he closed his eyes tightly.

"He has," Barnabas replied, "and we are on our way to dispose of his body outside the city gates."

"Let me see the body."

"Let me see the color of your money," Barnabas replied, his voice increasing in volume so that Sebastian could hear each word, "and wherein lies the beauty in gazing on a dead child?"

"I must needs see the body," Brother Sigismund insisted, "so I can be certain the deed is done."

"Very well, then, feast your eyes on the dead child."

Barnabas emphasized the last two words and Sebastian lay as still as he could, for he understood instinctively that were he found to be alive by Brother Sigismund it would not bode good. He could feel the impassive eyes alight on himself for his head was partly visible under the straw. Had he not felt those eyes often? It was at this point in time that a mouse ran out of the straw directly over his face, its little feet scurrying across his cheeks with a purposeless hurry. Sebastian did not breathe - he had gone numb - and continued to lie motionless.

"The rats will have him before the earth swallows him," Brother Sigismund remarked, as the rodent sped away.

Satisfied that the child was dead, he tossed a bag of coins to Peter, adding, "So I would advise you to inter him quickly."

Barnabas did not answer but pulled at the reins. The donkey obediently began to clop forward.

They passed out of the monastery lane onto the bigger road. Sebastian half sat up. Then the cart turned left.

Not a word had been spoken since they had left Brother Sigismund behind, but of a sudden Barnabas turned and looked directly at Sebastian. The pale glow of morning light colored the horizon.

"How are you, boy?"

The words were kindly spoken and had no venom in them. At that moment Sebastian placed the voice. It was the voice of the red-haired farmer, the man who had been angry with him for fingering the straw to clean the fish. It was the man whom Frau Kruger had addressed as Barnabas. His big hands held the reins lightly and he actually grinned at Sebastian who had slivers of straw sticking out of his hair.

"You played the role of corpse right well, lad. I'm proud of you."

Sebastian now sat up all the way. Brushing the straw off his clothes and out of his hair, he knew not what to say. He was lost in a world of events and questions that surpassed him.

"You must be confused," Barnabas went on, "and I can understand that. So I will tell you a story."

As he spoke, he patted the seat between himself and Peter. Peter who had not contributed a word to the conversation, turned at this point and extended a work-worn hand to Sebastian.

"Come, boy, sit between us. It'll warm you up and the truth is that I've never sat next to a corpse before"

After he said this, he began to laugh uproariously. Sebastian shakily stood up and was helped onto the wagon seat by the men. They drove in silence for a bit, the boy sitting awkwardly between the two, and then Barnabas began to tell his tale.

"I don't know how much you are aware of your parentage, young Sebastian, but I'll see if I can enlighten you a bit. Much of what I say will sound strange to your ears. But just listen. I worked for your father's family, you see, and was sent to be with your father when, as a young student he enrolled in a school in Regensburg. Regensburg lies east of Strasbourg. It is far away - some seventy leagues, I would venture to guess."

Sebastian felt as if he were living a dream. But he knew he was not in a dream for the donkey brayed mournfully and donkeys do not bray in dreams. From time to time the wagon bumped heavily along the road but Barnabas kept speaking. The boy was alternately thrown from the shoulder of Peter to the shoulder of Barnabas. He did not know what would happen to him. But he felt safe and was eager to learn where he came from.

"Your father was a fair student, not outstanding mind you, but not dull-witted either. As he studied, he became very much interested in the Jewish history of the area. He visited that section of Regensburg where the Jewish settlement had congregated in the very heart of the city, and he befriended a few of the families there. Isaac Neutel was one of the Jewish men he befriended and Isaac happened to have a daughter named Sarai. Sarai was dark-haired, very beautiful and full of laughter. It was not surprising that your father fell in love with her and she with him."

"Was this Sarai my mother?"

Sebastian's small voice interrupted Barnabas' saga.

"Yes, Sarai Neutel was your mother," Barnabas answered, "but both her family and your father's family were very much opposed to a marriage. They forbad it, especially in light of the fact that your mother had converted, along with your father, to the new Lutheran religion. But your father and mother ignored everyone's advice. They married and were very happy."

Sebastian stared at the donkey trotting along in front of the wagon. But within himself he saw a beautiful woman, a woman like Frau Kruger, with dark hair and a sweet face. The woman smiled at him and he smiled back. Barnabas' voice, next to him, broke in on his vision.

"Tensions between Christians and Jews were escalating in the city at this time. Jews were increasingly becoming the scapegoats whenever something went wrong in Regensburg. If, for example, the economy was poor, Jewish taxes were raised; and if someone became ill, the Jews were blamed with poisoning well water. It was not easy to be Jewish in Regensburg. And it was not an easy time for your father and mother but they loved each other deeply. Then the Emperor Maximilian I, died. Now it was under his administration that the Jews had enjoyed protection. After he died, the town council of Regensburg decided to expel all their Jews. The year was 1519. I will never forget it for as the days and weeks passed, all the Jews were forced to leave the town and their streets and homes were plundered."

The story sounded rather complicated to Sebastian and there was much that he did not comprehend. But he did want to ask one question.

"Did my mother and father leave Regensburg?"

"When these troubles began to get serious your father left and he left by himself. He had personally been threatened with death because he had married a Jew and your mother strongly urged him to go. She thought she would be safe in her parent's home, and she was sure the troubled times would pass. She finally convinced him to leave by having me promise that I would stay to guard her."

Barnabas halted his story and Sebastian was quick to ask, "And did you guard her?"

"When riots broke out in the streets and many were killed, I hid her. Then your father returned. But upon entering Regensburg he was caught up in a riot and hurt rather badly. He later died of these injuries. At this point, I took your mother and guided her out of the city. It was difficult but God was with me. Sebastian, there is another thing. Your mother was blind. She could not see."

Barnabas, whose voice had been terse in relating these last events, paused so long that Sebastian nudged him.

"Then what happened?"

"I took your mother to Strasbourg to her husband's family. But the sad story is that her deceased husband's family would not take her in. Her own family had all perished and so she was alone - all alone safe for me."

Barnabas again stopped for a moment and Sebastian noted that they were now driving towards the Judengasse, the street which he had visited but yesterday. It seemed an eternity ago. Again the boy prodded Barnabas.

"Then what happened?"

"I took your mother to my father's farm. You were born there a few months later. Your mother was very proud of you. But she was also very downhearted, very sad that she could not offer you more than a poor home. As I said, I had taken her to my father's farm. It was a peasant's home, Sebastian. I could provide nothing but a roof over her head and food on her plate. Then one day she was gone and she had taken you with her."

"Where did she go and how could she go by herself? She could not see."

"She must have bribed someone to take her to the Dominican monastery. And once there she must have somehow convinced the prior and brother Sigismund that you were heir to a small fortune. I know she did possess some valuable jewelry. She wanted very much for you to have an education."

Barnabas fell silent again. The donkey clip-clopped along and dawn was beginning to cast rosy hues over the gables of the houses they were passing.

"But what happened to my mother? Did she stay in the monastery too?"

"No, such a thing would not have been permitted."

"Then where did she go."

Barnabas turned his head and sadly regarded the young boy sitting next to him.

"I found her body a few days later. It was lying in one of the outer fields close to our property. She was dead, Sebastian. We supposed at the time that she had lost you somewhere, and that you were also dead."

Sebastian clasped and unclasped his hands. There were so many new things to think about.

"Do you not wonder what your father's name was, Sebastian?"

He shook his head. Indeed, he had not thought about it at all.

"It was Kruger - Johannes Kruger."

He did not know what to say to this information. Strange indeed that his father's last name should be the same as Frau Kruger's name.

"Your father was the brother of Philip Kruger - the same Philip Kruger who is married to the woman you met at the market."

Sebastian could not grasp the implications very quickly.

"This means," Barnabas went on, "that Philip Kruger is your lawful uncle. It means that you may come and live with him and Frau Kruger."

"But," Sebastian said slowly, "my father's family did not want my mother. Why should they want me?"

"When your mother arrived in Strasbourg, your uncle Philip was not home. He was gone on a business trip and absent for several months. When he later heard that his brother's wife Sarai had not been welcome, he was very angry with his parents. He actually traveled to Regensburg and searched for your father, not believing that he was dead. And much later he also came to our farm, but I could not tell him any more than I just told you. That your mother had died, and that we believed you to be dead also."

Sebastian sat quietly, watching the slow-moving feet of the donkey. A donkey, he reflected, had an easy life. He just ate, slept and pulled a cart.

"Frau Kruger sent a message to me after you visited her yesterday afternoon. Indeed, she was close to birthing, but she gave strict orders that you were to be followed and watched. She bears no great liking for the Dominicans and was worried that you might suffer consequences for visiting her. She also remarked on the strong resemblance you bore to the portrait they have of Johannes, your father. She wanted you to come home, Sebastian."

Sebastian could see himself standing on the stairs, staring up at the picture.

A flock of geese flew overhead. They honked and their wingspread fell on his ears.

"Frau Kruger did not know, and I did not tell her, that Brother Sigismund wanted you dead and had asked Peter here to do that job for him."

Peter slapped Sebastian's knee.

"He's a sly one, that Sigismund. He said you were worth nothing to him, never would be worth anything, and that you had more than eaten up the money your mother had given him for your keep."

"And now you are home, Sebastian," Barnabas said.

They had stopped in front of the large, half-timbered house. Dawn had fully broken now. Sebastian gazed in wonder at the steps leading to the front door.

"Is this true what you have told me?"

"It is true, lad."

And the wonder of it all filled Sebastian with a strangeness, a newness and a great gladness.

They climbed the steps and Barnabas knocked loudly on the front door, holding Sebastian in front of himself. Anna answered, even as she had answered but a day before. Her cap was askew, and her apron crumpled, but the smile on her face encompassed Sebastian standing at the threshold.

"A child has been born. And all is well," she exclaimed.

And Sebastian knew deeply within himself that this was, indeed, true and that all was well.

But the Blameless

Whoever misleads the upright into an evil way will fall into his own pit, but the blameless will have a goodly inheritance. (Prov. 28:10)

She wore a beret. It was no ordinary beret but one coquettishly adorned with a rose-colored feather on the left and layered with small, fine pearls along the edge. Walking around to the side of the bed, she held out her hand to him and he stretched out his own to encompass her slim, white fingers. But then the pain racked his body again and he winced, forced to shut his eyes, and when he opened them again she had vanished. A moment later he was uncertain whether or not she had actually been there.

"Renata?"

The whisper was hoarse and barely discernible. How long had he been in bed?

His voice did not carry beyond the sheets covering his aching, weary body. Where was his man-servant? He tried to recall why he was in bed; why he was so sore and so very tired. A bell tolled. Was it Sunday? There were steps outside in the street below. He could hear them clearly now. The steps were mingled with wailing and weeping. And then he remembered. The plague had come to the city. It had entered

Ellenberg in the year of our Lord 1527 and it had visited his house.

He closed his eyes, remembering more. Many of the German noble houses in Ellenberg had been devastated and his was one of the few which had remained untouched. He had forbidden Renata, the children and the servants to leave the premises. Things were wretched outside. But they had been wretched for several months and he had been quite sure that the plague was finally abating; he had been thoroughly convinced that his household had been spared due to his forethought. He had taken many precautions. Locking up the doors and lower windows of his house had been one of them, although the horrible smoke of the plague powder, burnt in many places, could be smelled right through the walls. Sustenance for which he paid dearly, had only been brought in through baskets let down by long ropes from the upper windows. He clearly recalled drawing up bread and beer; he could still feel the tension on the cord as he reached to lift the baskets. Had it been yesterday that he had last done so? Painfully his memory brought to mind how he had called out to the children that it was meal time and he distinctly saw himself carrying that last full basket to the drawing room only to find Renata stretched out on the floor. He had dropped the wicker container and had knelt down.

"Renata?"

She had only been able to whisper in reply. It was an apology.

"I was very careful, Johann. I did everything you said. We received no one. I did not go out. But ...."

The voice he so loved lost what strength it had left. There was death in her face. He had lifted her up and had carried her to a couch.

"Hush. I will send for a doctor."

But even as he spoke, he had known that it would be next to impossible to find either a doctor or an apothecary. Many had left the city, and of the ones still available few were willing to risk their lives by coming into contact with plague victims.

"The children?"

Next to death there was fear in her face and she had tried to say more but could not. He had patted her hand and had noted with great unease the pallor and the drops of sweat which stood out on her forehead. And yet only a few short hours before she had seemingly been well.

"I will go and check the children."

Stopping by the kitchen to call Trude, one of the maids, to attend to Renata, he had found the girl in the process of packing her possessions into a bundle.

"I'll not be staying."

"You knew the mistress was unwell and did not call me?"

"The children also ...."

She did not finish, but her hands trembled visibly. Nodding farewell, and not bothering to tie her bundle securely, the girl had half-run towards the outside kitchen door. Unlocking it, she had glanced back at him over her shoulder.

"Goodbye, sir. I'm only following Hans, Sophia and Hendrick who left half an hour ago."

Then she was gone from his home, gone from his threshold, running out into the street. The rest of the staff had left half an hour ago? What had he been doing that he had so missed the events of the day. Reading in his study? He had followed Trude over to the door, fully intending to lock it behind the girl. But he had opened it instead and had stared after her. Then he had called out loudly to the retreating figure as she sped over the cobblestones.

"See if you can find and send a doctor, Trude. Or," he had added quietly to himself, "anyone."

It had been late afternoon when Trude left. With a sigh he had closed the kitchen door and locked it fast again. Although what for? The plague had come in and it had come in through locked doors. Suddenly in a panic, remembering Trude's words, he had run up to check the children's bedroom. But death is no respecter of persons. There is equality of all in the fact and face of death – equality for mothers, children, and babies. He had gagged at the door of the nursery. For he had been able to tell at a glance that they were gone, that both his children were gone. Four-year-old Martin was stretched out in his crib with his arms above his round head, eyes wide open, staring at nothing. And two-year-old Amelia was curled up next to him. Slowly, foot over foot, he had come closer. Gently he had closed Martin's eyes, had fondled Amelia's hand. They were cold, his children. He had woodenly picked up a blanket and covered them. But what for? Soon the grave-bearers would come calling. They threw sand against his windows each evening and each evening he opened the casement and called out that all was well, that they need not bother, for all inside his home were still alive and well. But he had not been able to call out that all was well that evening.

Later, he had followed the corpse-bearers, those who pushed the carts with the dead bodies in them, to the cemetery. They had cautioned him to stay home but he could not. Like a magnet he had followed the men from a distance, and like a magnet his eyes could not pull away from the swaying bodies heaped atop one another in the carts. Then, a mile outside the city gates, they had reached the cemetery. Actually it was not really a cemetery; it was simply a trench dug out of necessity. There were not enough grave-diggers to dig individual graves for the innumerable corpses, corpses like those of his Renata, his Martin and his Amelia. The trench, which was really a circular hole, held a lot of bodies and they were all piled on top of one another. Leaning against a tree, he had watched from a short distance. Shovelful after shovelful of dirt were heaped on top of the dead – on his wife and on his children. There had been nothing he could do to prevent it. He had recalled a gravestone epithet he had once read when he had visited Nuremberg in the south. *Fourteen hundred and thirty-seven*, the gravestone year had read. And underneath the year, *Was that not sad and painful to relate, I died with thirteen of my house on the same date?* After weeping for hours, he had fallen asleep on the cold earth. In the early morning hours he had plodded home again through the shadow streets, feeling like a shadow himself. Once home, he had begun to feel ill and presuming it to be the plague, had

rifled through the closets for the death cloths he and Renata
had always kept ready. Many people kept linen burial cloths
in readiness for death. It was the cloth you were sewn into
before being interred. He had not sewn his Renata, or his
children into these cloths and felt ashamed that he had not.
But an unearthly weariness had taken hold of him those
awful hours. And yet he had gotten a death cloth for himself.
It lay now, at the foot of his bed, and he beheld its whiteness
outlined against the backdrop of the wooden bed boards.

Had this all happened yesterday? – or had it happened the
day before? He could not recall. How long had he lain in bed?
How long had he slept? His eyes closed again and he dozed.
He dozed and dreamt that he was extremely thirsty.
Consequently, he cried aloud for water.

"Give me water! Please, just one drop of water! One drop,
please!"

But no one offered him any water. And yet, for one
moment he became strangely aware of some movement by
the door. He vaguely saw someone outlined against the open
bedroom doorway holding what seemed to be a long pole.
Johann strained against the bed sheets, trying to lift his head
to ascertain what or whom it was. He was very hot and
remained extremely thirsty. He groaned out loud, raised his
right hand and whispered. "Please, please help me. I am so
thirsty."

The whisper barely left the bed and he could not tell
whether it reached the figure at the door. But the pole moved.

It moved across the room and became suspended over the bed. He could see it clearly now. A ferule, a long-handled spoon, was attached at its end. As he looked up at it, Johann saw that the host, the sacrament of the church, lay within the confines of the spoon. He was vaguely discomfited by its presence. In the first place, his mind grasped the fact that someone thought he was about to die; and in the second place, he did not want the proffered bread but desired water. More than anything else he wanted something to wet his lips, to soothe his dry throat.

"Water."

The whisper was even fainter this time. The spoon touched his cheek and moved towards his mouth. Johann's right hand, in a motion of weak, forlorn anger, pushed it away. There was a gasp from the doorway.

"He has touched the host."

Johann instantly recognized the voice. It was that of his step-brother, Gunther. He had not seen Gunther for over a year. There had been anger over the inheritance that his father had left them. He, the eldest, had been given the house in Ellenberg and some of the rentable property outside the city, whereas Gunther had been given a sizable sum of money which he had, so rumor had it, quickly squandered in riotous living. What was Gunther doing here, in his house, at this time? Johann's head hurt and he closed his eyes. And then everything became dark, dark as the sky without a moon and stars, dark as life without Renata and the children.

When Johann next opened his eyes, it was light outside. Indeed, it was so bright that his eyes refused to stay open.

Then a stench, a terrible stench, surrounded and filled his being. Like pungent smelling salts, it refused to let him sleep any longer. Lying flat on his back, he suddenly became aware that something was stretched out across his legs. It was heavy. Where was he? Trying to move, he became away that his arms as well were hampered by something massive. And why was it that the ceiling of his bedroom had a hole in it through which he could blink at the gleaming sky. Where was he? Turning his head, he stared into a dead man's distorted face. He was lying next to and under a corpse – a deceased man whose body was spilled half-way across his own. Horror overwhelmed him and he screamed. Given powerful impetus and strength through panic and dread, he flung off the load of dead flesh and sat up.

"Impatient grave-diggers," he yelled hoarsely, "and impatient grave! I do not yet come! No, I do not yet come!"

Pulling himself out of the tangle of dirt and arms and legs which seemed to be everywhere, he crawled. He crawled over scores of corpses – over patricians, peasants, bakers, tailors, maids, servants, priests and beggars. Lurid death greeted him at every motion of his creeping arms and legs, but he did not stop to speak back. He moved as quickly as he could. The flaccid, stinking bodies underneath him, many upon whom rigor mortis had already set in, did not deter him, could not stop him, and he reached the perimeter of the death circle in a few minutes time. Without glancing back, he kept inching along, kept going on all fours until he collapsed.

Johann slept. Or perhaps, as he later reflected, he lost consciousness. Partially aware before he hit the ground that he had reached the edge of a clump of trees, darkness engulfed him.

It was the smell of roasting meat and the sound of a crackling fire which awoke him. He savored the smell without opening his eyes. Perhaps it was a dream and he wanted it to last. Then he heard someone singing. It was a very soft singing and he could barely make out the words.

Ein' feste Burg ist unser Gott,
Ein gute Wehr und Waffen;

Turning his head ever so slightly in the direction of the sound, he opened his eyes and saw a young lad of perhaps seventeen or eighteen summers, turning what looked to be a rabbit on a spit atop a healthy fire. He studied the boy for a while. He was dressed simply in a doublet of brown cloth with sleeves, and a jerkin of the same color overtop. Dark hose was fastened by points to the doublet. All in all, it was a modest attire, so surely the boy was not wealthy. But certainly he was of a cheerful disposition. He looked kindly and alternately hummed and sang as he turned the animal round and round on the fire.

Mit unsrer Macht is nichts getan,
Wir sind gar bald verloren;
Es steit't für uns der rechte Mann,
Den Gott hat selbst erkoren.

Johann's right leg suddenly cramped and he moaned. The boy turned his head and smiled.

"So you are awake?"

He was at Johann's side in an instant, kneeling and looking earnestly at him. Johann said nothing, but only stared at the boy who loosened a flask attached to the upper rim of his waist-belt.

"I think you might be thirsty."

And then, with the utmost care, the boy put an arm under Johann's head, eased it up and put the mouth of the flask to his lips. Johann drank slowly and it seemed to him that he had never before tasted anything so sweet as the draught of water which the boy was now giving him to drink.

"Thank you."

The words came haltingly and Johann was amazed at the sound of his own voice. Then remorse shook him. Here was a boy, a boy on the verge of manhood, who was risking his life to help him.

"I've got the plague," he said, "and you will surely also die of infection if you don't leave me be. You best needs be on your way and leave me here."

"I think not," the boy replied cheerfully, "I've seen lots of people die of the plague and you've none of the symptoms. No boils, no smell, no dementia – no, I think you've had a bout of fever and bad luck perhaps. At any rate, I'm sure that in a few days you'll be feeling much better."

"Not the plague?"

"That's right," the boy said, "and how do you feel about chewing on a bit of rabbit?"

"What is your name?"

"Reinhardt Zolder. And what is yours?"

"Johann Eiser."

"Well, Johann, I am happy to make your acquaintance."

"How did you find me?"

The boy had turned back to the fire and became engaged in taking the rabbit off the spit. He glanced over his shoulder at the older man and laughed.

"It was not difficult. My horse, Old Swift, who is as good a horse as you'll ever see, almost stumbled right across you as you lay on the path we were following to Magdeburg."

"Why did you not leave me there to die?"

The look of surprise on the boy's face was obvious.

"Leave you to die? Why should I do that? I should hope that had I been in your place that someone would have helped me."

Johann pondered the words as he watched the boy put the rabbit on a bed of leaves before cutting it to pieces with a knife which he also took from his waist-belt.

"My wife and children died of the plague," he presently said softly, more to himself than to Reinhardt.

He suddenly lost his ravenous appetite as graphic images of the home he had tried to build in Ellenburg for Renata and the children came to his mind. It was an empty home now, and a home in which he had only lived for about a half a year. He remembered his brother's sudden appearing at his bedside and wondered if Gunther had been responsible for having the grave-diggers carry him to the death trenches.

Gunther certainly stood to inherit much. There were no other near relatives on father's side. But what did it matter anyway? The loneliness of the years to come suddenly brought nausea to his stomach and when Reinhardt brought some succulent bits of the rabbit over and sat down next to him to feed him, he turned his face away.

"Try one mouthful, Johann," the boy urged, "just one bite."

And because the lad had been so kind and had risked his life to take care of him, Johann turned his head and obediently opened his mouth as if he were a child. The brown meat was tender and moist, and in spite of himself Johann enjoyed the morsel.

"One more bite," the boy coaxed.

And he opened his mouth again. And so it was that Reinhardt nursed Johann back to health.

Ellenberg was a well-governed city. It had more than a two hundred and fifty streets which were cobbled and which were always kept clean. Dung hills were not allowed on these streets themselves, and was only permitted in certain corners. Neither was anyone allowed to throw any urine or other unclean material onto the street before ten of the clock at night. If this law was disobeyed, a fine of some 20 gulden besides possible imprisonment, was exacted. There were also rules about keeping pigs in one's backyard, and that was just until the animals were a half year old. The city was governed by a prudent Counsel of gentility. Because Sebastian had only resided there for less than half a year, he was not yet acquainted with many of these men. But on the whole, he had found it a very civil place to live. And he had been approved for citizenship by two members of the Counsel.

Johann slept much under the trees. His fever ebbed and waned, leaving him as weak as a kitten. He pondered his situation as he was slowly regaining his strength. If indeed, Gunther had seen to it that he had been carted down to the cemetery just outside the city gates, then Gunther would now be settling into his house and establishing ownership. He would not look kindly at his, Johann's, return. Sometimes Johann had no wish to return. At other times waves of anger overcame him at the murderous avarice of his half-sibling. At length, some ten days after being taken care of by Reinhardt, he persuaded the youth to go for a reconnaissance visit to Ellenberg. Instructing him carefully as to where his house was located, he bade the boy to knock at the door and to ask for Johann Eiser. If asked why, he was to answer that he had been offered, via a letter from Meister Eyk, a man whom Johann knew in Brunswick and from which place Reinhardt hailed, a position with the Eiser family as a servant.

"It is an untruth, you know," Reinhardt said initially.

"Yes, but it is to uncover truth," Johann answered.

The boy shrugged, agreed to go, walked over to his horse and mounted. The last Sebastian heard was the boy singing loudly as he rode his mare down the path to Ellenberg.

"Und wenn die Welt voll Teufel Wär'
Und wollt' uns gar verschlingen,
So fürchten wir uns nicht so sehr,

Es soll uns doch gelingen."

Reinhardt was of the new faith, as indeed many of the people in Ellenberg seemed to be. Johann did not think of himself as either Catholic or Protestant. Renata had leaned towards the new faith, and he had not hindered her.

It was quiet within the gates of Ellenberg but the worst of the epidemic was now over. Very few cases of plague had been reported the last week. Cautiously folks, the ones who had been left in the land of the living, were venturing back out onto the streets, and warily shutters were opened to let in a little sunlight. Reinhardt, who had been instructed well by Sebastian, had no trouble locating the Eiser residence in the Bonsard Straet. Tethering his horse to a post in front of the home, he climbed the stone steps and raised his hand to ring the great bronze bell that hung at the side. The ensuing noise startled him. The clanging seemed incongruous with the pervading silence of the streets. The sound had barely died down when the door opened and a man stared him in the face.

"Yes?"

"I have come," Reinhardt said, smiling at the man, "to speak with Johann Eiser."

"Johann Eiser?"

"Yes, is this not his residence?"

"Johann Eiser died of the plague some two weeks ago."

The man scrutinized him carefully as he spoke.

"He died?" Reinhardt repeated.

"Yes, I am his brother and know of a certainty that he died. If you had aught to say to my brother, you can also say it to me."

"Are you sure he died?" Reinhardt asked again.

"Yes, I am sure. I saw his body placed on the burial cart myself. Now what is it you wanted with him?"

It was clear that the brother was curious as to his business and Reinhardt, who had a sense of adventure as well as of truth, instantly decided to play that curiosity in his favor.

"I have a letter," he spoke falteringly, "but was told only to put it into Johann Eiser's hands. It is from some of his mother's kinfolk in Brunswick who desire to name him as beneficiary in their will."

He stopped. The brother licked his lips.

"Kinfolk?" he said, and added in his low and rather hoarse voice, "Will?"

"Yes," Reinhard continued, "but, of course, if you are a relative, a brother, you say, then I could perhaps ...."

He stopped again.

"Yes, of course you could," Gunther interrupted, stretching out a thin, bony hand, "Give it me, boy. Give me the letter."

"No," Reinhardt answered, stepping back on the stone platform in front of the door, "I could not in good conscience give you this letter unless ...."

"Unless what?"

"Well, unless you showed me proof positive that you were indeed his brother. Perhaps someone in the town Counsel could vouch for you."

"You simpleton," Gunther retorted, "See you not that I answered the door of this residence? How think you I can live here were it not for the fact that I am Johann's brother. Come! Give me the letter."

He placed a black foot over the threshold towards the outside and came closer to Reinhardt. But Reinhardt now backed down the steps.

"I will be back tomorrow," he said, "and if you can obtain proof positive that you are Johann Eiser's brother, I will hand you the letter."

Having said that, he hastily walked over to Old Swift, untied him, jumped onto his back and rode off.

"You are dead, friend," he told Johann who was sitting, back against an oak, in the noon sunlight, "as dead as a leaf blown off a tree in autumn."

"Am I?" Johann answered with a smile, "Well, we shall see about that."

"What shall you do?"

"Well, tomorrow I will ride into Ellenberg with you and confront Gunther. If two members of Counsel are indeed with him, they will confirm that I am Johann and that he is not legally permitted to live in my house without permission."

"Why did you simply not come with me today? Why did you not confront him directly?"

"Because, my dear young friend, don't you see? It is obvious that Gunther wants me dead. Otherwise, why would he have placed me on the death cart? Neither would he have confessed to being there when I was placed on the death cart. He had a hand in my so-called 'death'. He tried to get rid of me by unsavory means and I think he would not hesitate to do so again. He was ever a spoiled and wilful child."

Reinhardt was silent.

"Should you not give him a chance? I grant you he did not make a good impression on me, but perhaps he really did think you were dead. Perhaps he had no hand in ...."

"You are young, my friend, and very naive. I will not hesitate to report my half-brother to the Ellenberg Counsel as a liar and a cheat and a would-be murderer."

"I just think," Reinhardt tried again, "that you...."

Again he was interrupted.

"No, my friend. I know you mean well, but in this instance you are wrong. I owe you my life and would listen to you on a number of topics, but on this one. No!!"

While he was speaking, Johann suddenly stood up. Perhaps too suddenly. He began shaking, not only with the emotions he had undergone the last two weeks, but also with the exertion of his body. The exercise caused his still weak legs to buckle under him and he was forced to hang onto the trunk of the tree under which he had been recuperating.

"You are not well yet."

Reinhardt spoke softly and solicitously. Johann nodded and sat down again, leaning wearily against the bark.

"One more night's good sleep and one more good meal prepared by your hand, shall see me a great deal closer to being well."

Cheeks flushed, breathing heavily, he closed his eyes. After watching him for a lengthy while, and making sure that he had fallen asleep, Reinhardt walked over to his horse and sprang back into the saddle. It might well be possible to visit Ellenberg and be back before dark; back before Johann would wake.

For the second time that day, Reinhardt stood in front of Johann's home and rang the great bronze bell. And for the second time that day, the door was opened. But this time it was not Gunther who faced Reinhardt but a stocky fellow, not a burgher, but a peasant judging by his attire.

"I've come to see Gunther Eiser."

"What about?"

"That I will tell him when he comes to the door."

There was a commotion in the hall behind the peasant. The man shrugged his broad shoulders.

"You have your wish. Here he is."

He moved aside and Reinhardt looked into the heavily lidded eyes of Sebastian's brother once again.

"Why are you back? Did you change your mind and decided to give me the letter today after all?"

He smiled ingratiatingly and went on.

"A wise decision, by all means, and one that will be rewarded."

In spite of all his goodwill, Reinhardt felt a trickle of revulsion run through him. The man had something about him, something shady. Nevertheless, that did not mean he had committed murder and perhaps, upon learning that Johann was still living, he would be overjoyed.

"I have come back," he began, "to tell you...."

"Wait," Gunther smiled, revealing broken teeth.

Extending a hand to Reinhardt, he continued, "Wait before you continue and step inside. You must indeed be tired and I am a bad host not to have offered you, as I ought to have done when you last came here, a draught of ale."

Uncertain as to whether or not the man was sincere, Reinhardt took the extended hand and hesitatingly stepped inside over the threshold. The other man stood back in the hall way and then disappeared into the shadows of an alcove.

"Just walk on, friend," Gunther's low, gravelly voice spoke up behind Reinhardt, "just walk on and turn to the right. We'll sit in the kitchen, if that is to your liking, for that is where the ale is kept and that is where it is most comfortable."

Reinhardt turned as directed and entered a large room. A great wooden table stood in the middle of the room, and two high-backed chairs straddled the long ends. Gunther sat in one of these and gestured that Reinhardt should sit in the other. He did so and the peasant who had softly walked in behind them, placed a flagon in front of Gunther. Then he opened a cupboard and took out three cups. He did not speak, but he did give Reinhardt a curious look, appraising him, before pouring out what seemed to be a wine, into all three of the cups. He placed one in front of Reinhardt and another in front of Gunther. The third he appropriated for himself. Then he stood back, looking expectantly at Gunther.

"Drink up, my friend," Gunther said as he lifted his cup, "Here's to friendship and to health."

"To health," Reinhardt answered as he lifted up his cup, bringing it to his lips.

The ale was sweet, and he had been thirsty. But there was a bitter aftertaste to the drink. "Now then," Gunther spoke as he leaned back in his chair, "what is it that you have come to tell me?"

"I have come to tell you," Reinhardt spoke, "that Johann, your brother, is not dead as you suppose. He is alive and well and ...."

He stopped, staring at Gunther. The man had turned pale and had gotten up from his chair.

"What is it that you are saying?" he demanded as he began to stride around the table, "What lies are you spreading?"

"No lies," Reinhardt responded, rising as well, but feeling a little unsteady as he repeated, "No lies."

He thought it passing strange that the floor seemed to be sliding away from under his feet and that the ceiling seemed to be falling down straight on top of him. And then everything disappeared.

****

It was mid-afternoon of that same day when Johann awoke. It took a few moments before he recalled his last conversation with Reinhardt. Where was the boy? There was no fire in the round pit where the lad was wont to cook supper; neither were there any good aromas wafting over to tell him that another pheasant, hare or fish had been caught with which to tempt his appetite. Had the young man been upset or angry with him? No, that would not be like him at all. Reinhardt was too good-natured for such petty feelings. Perhaps he was still out hunting and had not had much success today. He leaned back against the tree and closed his eyes again for a moment, thinking. This was the first time that Reinhardt had not been present at the campsite when he awoke. Wait! Was the horse gone? Usually Reinhardt hunted on foot in and around the small copse they had called home this past while. He stood up slowly and turned his eyes towards the place where the horse was usually tethered. There was no animal there. He went over to the fire pit, and sat down on the edge. Slipping his hand into a pile of leaves at the edge, he drew out a leather bottle containing sweet wine. Reinhardt kept it there for medicinal purposes. So he had told Johann anyway. Taking out the cork, he lifted the bottle to his lips and took a good, long drink. Now where could Reinhardt be? He no longer felt light-headed, but quite fit. The thought suddenly struck him that, considering the fact that the boy had been upset about reporting Gunther to the Counsel, he might have traveled back to Ellenberg by himself to ... to what? What could he do or say to anyone that would change the situation? Of course, Reinhardt had given Gunther the benefit of a doubt. It was his nature to think the best of everyone. A pang of doubt assailed him as well but he squelched it. Had not Gunther grieved his mother and sent her to an early grave by his philandering? Had he not continuously pestered their father for money and more money? And had he not been forbidden entrance to several towns because of suspicion of theft? Not that anyone had ever been able to prove anything, but the trail of unpaid bills, of angry landlords and of cuckolded husbands was endless.

Johann stared out into the distance. The sun was setting. He instinctively felt that Reinhardt would not return, not that evening, at any rate. If he walked to town now, even on foot, he could probably still enter before the gate was locked for the night and knock on the Burgermeister's door. And so Johann began his journey back to Ellenberg.

It was as Johann had thought. Just as darkness was beginning to fall in earnest, he reached the gate. The walk had actually done him good and although he was tired, it was a healthy sort of tiredness. He located the Gassen Straet without any difficulty and hoped that the Burgermeister was in residence, that he had not left the city during the plague epidemic. His knocking was answered by a major-domo, the chief steward, dressed in an embroidered jacket with a stiff, high collar.

"Is Herr Mutzer, the burgermeister, at home?"

"Yes, but he is not seeing visitors presently. Please come back in the morning."

"No, I must see him now. I have an urgent matter to present to him that cannot wait."

The major-domo laughed, but it was a humorless laugh.

"There are many urgent matters. One of them is that the Burgermeister lost his wife and his children these past weeks, and he is not in a state to be disturbed during this time of the evening."

"Who is it, Elias?"

The voice of the burgermeister, tired but authoritative, rang through the hallway.

"It is I, Johann Eiser, your worship. I have come to see you on a matter of some import, but ...."

Johann paused. He really did not know Herr Mutzer very well. How would he be received?

"Send him in, Elias."

The conversation Johann had with Herr Mutzer was easier than he had supposed it would be. Having lost a wife and children himself, the Burgermeister was very sympathetic. He promised to go to the Eiser residence with Johann first thing in the morning, and offered him a bed for the night. Then he excused himself and retired, leaving Johann in the care of the major-domo, a dour man of few words but one who made sure that he was properly fed and made comfortable.

True to his word, the Burgermeister escorted Johann to his home the next morning. As well, two members of the City Counsel and two members of the City Guard had been notified. Four men consequently accompanied Johann and Herr Mutzer. The first thing that Sebastian noted, upon sighting his home, was that Reinhardt's horse was tethered to a post in front of the house. He pointed it out to the Burgermeister, who nodded.

"It's best if you go ahead by yourself, Johann, and ring the bell. We will wait here within full view and earshot."

Climbing the steps, hand on the iron guard railing, Johann pondered how strange life was. It seemed like yesterday that he had been coaxing Amelia to jump down from these very steps into his arms, and that little Martin had been cheering her on. And Renata ... Renata had stood at the top step smiling at her family, smiling at the children and himself. But she was no more and he stood here alone now. Automatically his hand went up to ring the bronze bell. But the effort was only half-hearted now and the noise was pathetically soft compared to the memories that now assailed him with clarion tones. Yet, in spite of the diminutive sound of the bell, the door opened almost immediately. A rather unsavory stocky man stared him in the face.

"Yes?"

"I've come to see Gunther Eiser."

"Herr Eiser is not available right now."

"Can you please tell him that his brother has come to see him."

"His brother is dead."

"His brother is very much alive. I am he."

"You had better be gone or I will call the City Guard."

The threat got no further for at a motion from the Burgermeister, who had been carefully following every word, the two attending members of the City Guard strode forward and up the steps.

"Here is the Guard," Johann said, "as well as Herr Mutzer, the Burgermeister, and two members of the City Counsel. Now you had better step aside to let me in, I think, and you had also better call Herr Gunther Eiser."

The man turned a trifle pale, a pale apparent even under his brown, sun-burned face.

"I am only a passing stranger, by the name of Lud Martin," he faltered, as he edged his way towards the open door, "I am an honest man who sought refuge here for the night, refuge which Herr Eiser was kind enough to provide. Not wishing to interfere in family matters, I beg leave to excuse myself from this conversation and will continue my journey through to ...."

He was not able to finish his sentence, as the Guard prevented him from leaving the house and walking down the steps.

"Please walk through," the Burgermeister said as he tapped Johann on the shoulder.

He had positioned himself behind his protégé. Disdainfully eyeing Lud Martin, he continued in an authoritative voice.

"We will ascertain whether or not either your brother or your young friend is present. If not, we shall have to send out a search party."

Johann walked on through the hallway and turned to the right, making for the kitchen. He had heard, or thought he heard, some small commotion there while they were speaking by the front door. Opening the kitchen door, he came face to face with Gunther who eyed him warily but not with fear. Reinhardt was lying on the floor on a blanket.

"Sebastian!" Gunther cried out loud, clapping his hands as he did so, "What a blessing to see you alive, you whom I had thought dead! I will pray to the blessed Virgin ...."

He stopped, taking note of the small group of people congregated behind Johann in the hallway.

"And who are these people with you?"

Johann did not bother to answer but, pushing Gunther aside, immediately strode over to where Reinhard lay.

"What have you done to him?" he demanded as he advanced across the kitchen floor.

"Done?"

Astonishment was increasingly apparent in Gunther's low, smooth voice as he repeated the word.

"Done? Why nothing, dear brother. The fellow came to my door last night and wished to speak with me. I think he said it was about a personal matter. Maybe I am too trusting but I invited him in, as any civil person should, and offered him some wine. He swallowed the contents of the flagon so quickly that I gave him a second pouring, judging him to be parched after perhaps traveling a long way. But, in truth, I think he was not used to any wine for straightway he became so muddle-headed and sleepy that I let him lie down on the floor where he has slept until now."

Sebastian, kneeling down next to Reinhardt, gently slapped the boy's face.

"Wake up, Reinhardt, lad. Wake up."

Reinhardt moaned softly.

"He will have a small headache, I think, and likely some nausea from imbibing the wine," Gunther continued.

Reinhardt's eyes opened. They were slightly glazed.

"Reinhardt, lad," Johann spoke, "are you all right?"

Reinhardt's eyes focused on Sebastian.

"Johann? How did you...? Where am I?"

He sighed deeply, shutting his eyes for a moment before he went on.

"I think I remember. Your brother gave me a drink. There was another man as well ...."

"You see," Gunther interrupted, "it is as I said."

"You were very free," Burgermeister Mutzer said, "with your hospitality last night, Gunther Eiser. That is to say, you were free with your brother's home, for it is not yours."

Gunther stared at the Burgermeister, not sure who the man was.

"I am the Burgermeister of Ellenberg, and I have come to see that ..."

"Oh, your Honor," Gunther interrupted him, "I am absolutely overcome with gratitude that my brother is here, that he is alive. I was overwhelmed by sadness at his supposed demise."

"Why is it that you had him taken by the corpse-bearers?"

"He had stopped breathing, Herr Burgermeister. A fact which can be verified by those who were on duty at the time."

"And what do you make of the fact that he is alive and standing in front of you? Had he died in the plague trench, his blood would have been required by God at your hands, Gunther Eiser."

A flicker of fear passed over Gunther's face. At least that is what Johann thought. But then it passed and the face was impenetrable once more.

"God knows my heart, sir. And I am quite willing to let Him judge me."

"And what say you, young Reinhardt?"

The Burgermeister now concentrated his gaze on Reinhardt, who was trying to sit up and succeeding with the help of Johann. The soldiers who were guarding Lud Martin, as well as the two counsel men, all stood congregated in the doorway of the kitchen.

"I do not know what to say, sir. I came here last night and after being asked in, was indeed offered a drink in this place, in this kitchen. I cannot remember too much after that."

"It is likely that Reinhardt would have ended up in the plague trench as well."

Johann spoke through clenched teeth and eyed Gunther with some malice.

"Not so, brother," Gunther responded with a smile, "why would I have wished to hurt this lad. Besides, my other visitor, Herr Martin, can verify every word I have spoken so far. Can you not Lud?"

Martin Lud shifted from one foot to the other. All eyes were on him. Turning his gaze downward and examining the tiled floor, he finally spoke.

"It is as Gunther says."

"Do you have anything to add? Do you wish to accuse Gunther of anything?" the Burgermeister once again addressed Reinhardt.

"No, sir. I am satisfied that I was overcome by wine. I do not think there was foul play involved."

Johann eyed his young friend with a mixture of pity and anger.

Reinhardt continued. "I think Johann, that you are free to move back into your home and that you can resume, or rather, begin your life anew."

"For your sake, Reinhardt, you who have saved my life, I will not press this matter about Gunther any further before the Counsel present here. Please understand that I respect your trust and will therefore," and he heavily emphasized the word 'therefore', "neither charge nor hinder my brother from leaving."

Here he looked pointedly at Gunther, who smiled coldly at him, bowed and asked permission to pick up his belongings from one of the bedrooms. It disgusted Johann to think that Gunther had actually slept in his home.

"Permission granted," he barked, "and then quit these premises as quickly as possible and don't let me see your face around here again."

"It is a misunderstanding," Gunther breathed, "After a month or so you will realize this. May God grant you peace and happiness, brother. May God grant you the ability to cope with your bereavement."

He walked towards the kitchen door. The group parted to let him pass and he made his way down the hall and up the stairs.

"You will not change your mind, young sir?" the Burgermeister asked Reinhardt.

"No," Reinhardt answered, "for I am not totally positive that he drugged me, or meant me any harm."

Johann made a derisive noise.

"Well, I will not contest your judgment," he said slowly, "for you have saved my life. I am not sure I am happy with this gift of home and hearth, but the truth is that I am glad that Gunther will not live in this place."

A thought suddenly struck him. Reinhardt was looking for work. He had told him so during the days he had nursed him. He had spoken of his hopes of gaining employment on a farm so that he could provide a home for his mother and sister who were living in Magdeburg with other relations. Well, why should he not give Reinhardt employment? As far as that went, why not allow him to take possession of some of the land that he owned just outside Ellenberg? Would that not be a good way of thanking the lad?

"I own a farm, Reinhardt," he began, "and am looking for a good tenant-farmer. The property is located just outside Ellenberg, to the south of it. It is, or has been standing vacant for some time, as the previous tenant died, even during my father's days. He was looking for someone to work it and I wonder...?"

The answering grin on Reinhardt's face was huge.

"You are too kind," he answered, his words spilling over with enthusiasm, "and I shall bring my sister and mother over from Magdeburg and I shall run the best farm you ever saw, Sebastian. You will not regret the investment."

"There is more," Johann said, "Reinhardt Zolder, in front of all these witnesses, which includes yourself, Herr Mutzer, Burgermeister of Ellenberg, I am not simply asking you to be a tenant-farmer, but I hereby give you the farm of which I am speaking, the deed of which I will shortly fetch from Herr Moltke on Rat Straet, who kept all such documents for my father and who now keeps them for me."

"You are giving the boy the farm?"

It was spoken from the hall-way. Gunther reappeared in the doorway even as all shifted over to make room for him.

"What is it to you?" Johann replied.

"It is our father's land. And, as such, should stay in our family."

"I am giving it to Reinhardt Zolder in the presence of all these witnesses and I will ask Herr Moltke to draw up the transfer of the land later this week. And that is the end of the matter."

But the way that Gunther stalked out, all knew that very likely it was not the end of the matter.

****

Within a year Ellenberg had returned to its usual activities. Many had lost loved ones but they accepted this as the inevitable. Times could be good and times could be bad. God ordained both. Widows and widowers alike remarried. Shops re-opened, produce was sold once more, and laughter and the sound of children returned to the streets. Reinhardt Zolder, as well as his mother and his sister, became a part of the Ellenberg community. They lived on good terms with the people with whom they came into contact, and were well-liked for their friendliness and piety. Although Reinhardt worked hard and long, he was reputed to be generous. Johann visited them often and many times the two of them could be seen walking together in deep discussion.

There was only one matter on which Johann and Reinhardt disagreed – and that was on the providence of

God. The fact that Reinhardt so readily put all into God's hands, that he was so trusting, both irritated and baffled Johann.

"It was my doing," he remonstrated with the young man, "that saved you from the clutches of Gunther, and my doing alone."

"Firstly," the boy replied, "you do not have undeniable proof that he was out to kill either of us, and secondly, you would not have been able to come, had not God permitted you to come."

"God helps those who help themselves," was the ready answer.

They were sitting at the kitchen table of the home which Johann had given to the Zolder family.

"And this farm," Johann went on, "surely you see that I have given you this farm. That I have helped you."

"Indeed," Reinhardt answered, "I am in your debt and your friend for life. But the truth is that God Himself, although through you, has blessed me exceedingly beyond my expectations. And I thank Him for it and praise Him."

Such a smile was on his face, that Johann felt shame. Reinhardt was of the new religion even as his Renata had been inclined. No popery for him, no candle burning, no indulgence buying or any such thing. It was all grace, grace and more grace, to hear him talk. All good and well, but a little thought and planning went a long way to see a man through this world and perhaps through the next as well. Truthfully, he could neither say nor see that Reinhardt did not think ahead. He planned his crops, his days, and all his time very carefully. But the lad was too trusting. It sometimes bordered on the realm of idiotic the way thata boy lent and gave freely, always saying that the Lord would provide.

"What of Gunther?" he said abruptly as Reinhardt made as if to get up.

"What of him?"

"Well, the talk is that he has been seen in town recently. There is also a rumor that he has been inciting certain riffraff in town against you."

"God will protect me. I have done nothing wrong."

Having said that, Reinhardt got up from the kitchen table.

"I must see to the animals in the stable."

He left and Johann remained, pondering, hands supporting his chin. Reinhardt's mother and sister came in a few moments later.

"Good-afternoon, Herr Eiser."

"Good-afternoon to you as well. But as I've told you before, please just call me Johann and not Herr Eiser."

He eyed them both women with pleasure. Frau Hildegard Zolder was a handsome woman in her early forties. Calm and confident in manner, she mothered him even as she mothered her own two children. Elza was a year younger than her brother, and a very beautiful girl. Indeed, he sometimes felt guilty at the delight he felt in the sweetness of her demeanor. He stood up.

"Well, I must be off."

"You will not stay to sup with us tonight?"

"No, not tonight. Another time soon. But thank you."

Herr Mutzer stopped Johann at the city gate.

"Johann Eiser, I have been waiting for you."

"For me? Why, what have I done?"

Herr Mutzer laughed.

"Done? Nothing, my friend. But I would like to have a private word with you at my home. Perhaps later today?"

"Fine."

They arranged for that evening and so it was that Johann and the Burgermeister sat opposite one another in the Burgermeister's study almost a year to the date of that time when Sebastian had first come to him for help.

"There has been talk about Reinhardt in the town and I thought...."

Herr Mutzer paused and shifted his position about on his chair.

"What did you think and what was the talk about?"

Johann was both puzzled and fiercely interested.

"Well, the talk was about his ... his background. It seems, you see, that there is Jewish blood in his veins and ...."

"Well, what if Jewish blood does run through his veins?"

Johann shrugged his shoulders indifferently as he spoke.

"Johann, you know as well as I do, that Jews are often blamed for disasters. Any disasters. And the last disaster here was the plague."

"But it is over. People are getting back to normal. Anyway, who is the one who is spreading vile rumors about Reinhardt?"

"As I was about to tell you, Gunther is back and ...."

Johann interrupted again.

"I knew he was back and I also knew he was inciting people against Reinhardt. But I didn't know what he was saying."

"Well, now you know."

"But people here are sensible," Johann retorted, "and besides that, Reinhardt and his mother and sister are well-liked. I don't think that anyone ...."

Now it was the Burgermeister's turn to interrupt.

"Perhaps not, Johann. But it is better to be forewarned."

"Yes," Johann replied thoughtfully, "but what shall we do with this information?"

The Burgermeister was not the only one who spoke to Johannn about Gunther's gossip and malicious ways. Hendrick, one of the man-servants Johann and Renata had previously had in their employ and one whom Johann had rehired, also warned his master.

"I was down at the Elk and Arms last night, sir," he began that very same evening, "and I heard one of the men there speak about Reinhardt in a very unfitting manner."

"How so," Johann inquired.

"It was with regard to Reinhardt being seen in Ellenberg prior to the plague. The man strongly hinted that Reinhardt might have poisoned the wells with something or other to make people catch the plague."

"Well, and did you put a stop to such nonsense talk?"

"Well, no, sir. I was outnumbered. The man who was slandering Reinhardt was one of five gathered around your brother who is back in town. They were a rough, ill-looking bunch. Truth be told, I don't even know if they were from our area."

"Hmm."

The low exclamation was all the response that escaped Sebastian's lips. But after a moment of reflection, he asked Hendrick a question.

"Do you know, or can you find out what exactly they plan to do?"

"I might be able to find out, sir."

"See that you do, Hendrick. And if you do, I shall reward you."

"No need to, sir. I've often regretted leaving you that time during the plague. Perhaps in this way I can ...."

Not letting him finish, Johann slapped him on the back.

"No need to go on. But be careful, Hendrick! My brother is a rogue and a scoundrel. He'll not stop at using force if someone stands in his way."

Hendrick smiled. He was a big and brawny man.

"I'll be careful, sir. But so should he."

Early the next day Hendrick unobtrusively stationed himself at the Elk and Arms. In a shaded corner of the large taproom he watched people coming in and people going out. Without fail, he kept an eye on customers the whole morning long. Mid-afternoon his vigilance paid off. He once more overheard a conversation by some of the same fellows whom he had seen with Gunther the previous night.

"I've saw the Jew coming into town on a wagon. The plan is to wait by ...."

The voice was hoarse and low. Hendrick couldn't quite make out where the conspirators planned to wait for Reinhardt, but there was no doubt, as he caught the next sentence, that their intentions were not friendly.

"Have you got the rope and the cudgels, Franz?"

Hendrick was sitting with his back towards the men, but he dared not at that moment turn his head, for fear that they would note his presence and stop talking. They were drinking rather heavily. He could hear noisy swallowing, belching and grunting noises. Carefully taking out some paper he had carried with him in his pocket, he wrote a small note to Master Sebastian, warning him that Reinhardt must be careful on his way home that evening. Some ten minutes passed before he deemed it safe to slowly stand up and make his way to the counter. There he was able to pass the note on to an errand boy with strict instructions to see it delivered immediately. Then, while not trying to appear too conspicuous, he walked back to the spot where he had been sitting.

Another hour or two passed. The men from which Hendrick had gleaned his information, stayed and continued to drink. Then, about an hour before dusk, they got up and departed. It was fast becoming dark. Not only because it was approaching the hour of dusk, but also because there was a storm in the making. A fierce wind rattled the inn's windows. Involuntarily, Hendrick shivered. It was definitely time to return to Master Johann to tell him that evil was in the offing and that Reinhardt had best plan to stay in Ellenberg overnight. He had no idea where the ruffians were planning to waylay Reinhardt. Hopefully he and Master Johann could persuade the young man to stay overnight. Then surely tomorrow, in the daylight, they would be able to confront these base fellows and .... His thoughts stopped. He was intelligent enough to know that the men could not be arrested on the basis of what they had said in perhaps a drunken moment. Nevertheless, he had better leave and allow Master Johann to make the decisions as to what would be the best course of action presently. There had been no one behind him for the last five minutes. He got up slowly and had almost reached the door of the taproom, when someone slapped him on the shoulder.

"Well, if it isn't Hendrick, servant-boy of brother Johann."

Turning quickly, he came face to face with Gunther.

"Gunther!"

"Yes, and that's Master Gunther to you, Hendrick."

The hand that still lay on his shoulder, pinched him hard and he winced. But he would not be coerced into a fight for that would mean that he would not be free to leave and speak to Master Johann.

"Out for a drink, were you?"

Ostensibly friendly, Gunther's eyes were cold and searching. Hendrick nodded.

"Yes, I was. And now, pray excuse me, I'm on my way out."

"He's not home, you know."

Gunther spoke softly, almost whispering into Hendrick's ear.

"Who's not home?"

"My brother and your employer, Johann Eiser."

"That remains to be seen, doesn't it?"

While speaking, Gunther had edged his way towards the door. Hendrick was but a step behind him. Gunther flung open the door, bowing and grinning malevolently.

"After you, dear Hendrick, after you."

Outside the sky was ominous. Huge storm clouds billowed across the sky. The wind was of such force that both men involuntarily clasped their cloaks with their hands and put their faces down.

At the precise moment that Hendrick and Gunther left the Elk and Arms, Reinhardt and Johann, seated on Reinhardt's wagon, were at the city gate.

"Do you not see by the weather that you ought to have stayed in Ellenberg? You know that I can put you up for the night. Why must you be so foolhardy as to persist in going home?"

"Precisely because of that. It is my home and mother and Elza will be watching for me. In this weather they are apt to be worried. And although I appreciate your company, you really need not have come along, Johann, my friend."

Johann grunted. He had received Hendrick's note, had paid the errand boy well and had immediately sought out Reinhardt whom he knew to be at the smithy.

"Well, I can see, even if you cannot, that two men together on such a night as this when not even a cat would venture out, are safer than one man alone."

"We are never really alone, Johann," Reinhardt rebuked the older man gently.

"Yes, yes, I know. But ...."

Lightning flashed in front of them, illuminating the road ahead with grotesque shadows.

"It is very dark. What makes you think you will be able to find your way home?"

Johann spoke lightly, but he was apprehensive.

"Old Swift knows the way, don't you girl?" Reinhardt replied, reaching forward to pat the horse's rump and clucking his tongue to manifest his trust in the beast's ability.

"I doubt she hears you in this din of wind and weather."

Reinhardt, who was extraordinarily fond of his horse, was slightly offended.

"Old Swift knows the road blind-folded, Johann. Were I to do nothing, she would find her way home without me telling her which way to turn."

"Nevertheless, I would appreciate it if you would guide the nag."

Johann was irritated. It had begun to rain. That, together with the wind, was beginning to make him rather miserable.

"I've a lantern in the back of the wagon. Reach behind you, Johann, and light it. It will make you more at ease, I think. Although I vow that I could just as easily ride in the dark. Old ...."

"Yes, yes, I know," Johann replied testily, "Old Swift is a wonder-horse."

He found the lantern and after considerable effort was able to light it with the tinderbox Reinhardt also provided.

For some miles they rode in silence. That is to say, the sound of the wind, and the distant rumbling of the thunder, reverberated through that silence. Eventually they reached a crossroads where a right turn must be made in order to reach the farm house. It was now only some six miles hence. Old Swift stopped at the intersection.

"Gee, Old Swift!! Gee, girl!!" Reinhardt called through the noise.

But like a balky mule, Old Swift suddenly refused to move, let alone turn right. She stayed where she was and no matter what Reinhardt said and no matter how hard he pulled on the reins, there was no movement.

"Clever horse, Old Swift, isn't she," Johann couldn't help shouting out in mock ridicule.

Although wet through and through, he found a certain satisfaction in seeing Reinhardt leap off the wagon to coax the horse with soft words, and getting absolutely no result. The thunder clapped. It was a lot louder than it had been a few moments before. Reinhardt leapt back on the wagon next to Johann.

"I don't know what's gotten into her," he pondered, "maybe she's spooked because of the storm. But the truth is that I've ridden through worse weather with her."

Suddenly the wagon did move. Not to the right, not towards the farmhouse where Hildegard and Elza were waiting by a warm hearth, but to the left. And not at a safe, easy trot, but at breakneck speed. Recklessly, Old Swift tore across the road. The lantern, which had been in Johann's hand but a moment before, plummeted to the wayside.

Immersed in darkness, both men gripped hard the edge of the wooden seat on which they were sitting.

"What," Johann gasped, as soon as he had recovered from the surprise, "has gotten into the animal, Reinhardt? Has she gone crazy?"

Reinhardt did not reply. Instead of slowing down after a few moments, as might be expected, Old Swift picked up on speed and seemed to be going faster by the minute. Wet rain stung Johann's cheeks. He turned it to look at Reinhardt, but could not make out even the contour of his companion's face. But he did hear, above the sound of the sweeping wind and the pelting rain, the strains of a song. The notes were not soft, but carried great volume. Indeed, he had not known that Reinhardt possessed such a powerful voice.

"Ein' feste Burg ist unser Gott,
Ein gute Wehr und Waffen;
Er hilft uns frei aus aller Not,
Die uns jetzt hat betroffen.

Reinhardt sang on with gusto but Johann closed his eyes. It seemed to him as if the wind was blowing clean through his bowels. A few minutes later, cautiously opening his eyes again, he sensed that perhaps, just perhaps, Old Swift was decelerating. But he still expected every minute to be his last. Then the wagon turned sharply to the right, axles groaning and wood creaking. And Reinhardt kept making music.

Mit unsrer Macht ist nichts getan,
Wir sind gar bald verloren;

Es steit't für uns der rechte Mann,
Den Gott hat selbst erkoren.
Fragst du, wer der ist?
Er heisst Jesu Christ,
Der Herr Zebaoth,
Und is kein andrer Gott,
Das Feld muss er behalten.

It was true, Johann surmised, even as he was enveloped by Reinhardt's words and baritone, they were slowing down. Not only that, they were actually coming to a complete stop.

"Where are we?"

"I have no idea," Reinhardt answered briefly, "none at all."

"What shall we do? Turn back?"

"It's too dark," Reinhardt said, "and the best thing we can do is to lay down under the wagon and try to sleep until daylight."

"Sleep?"

"Yes, why not. At any rate, under the wagon we will be drier than on top of the wagon."

"You don't think that Old Swift will take off again?"

"I'll undo her harness and that way...."

He didn't finish his sentence, but jumped down, quietly approaching the horse. Foam flecked the mare's mouth and she moved her head back and forth.

"Hey there, old girl," Reinhardt said, "what happened back there to make you gallop as if the butcher was after you with his knife? Oh well, you've carried me for so many years, that I'll not complain this one time."

"Well, I will," Johann called out still sitting on top of the wagon, "and if Old Swift was a man, I'd cuff him between the ears."

Having said this, he also jumped down and after a sigh, crawled under the wagon. Reinhardt joined him there a moment later.

"We could have stayed home," Johann whispered, "and none of this would have happened."

"God knows," Reinhardt answered.

And the rain fell on the wagon that whole night.

The sun shone faintly that next dawn and both Johann and Reinhardt were enormously surprised to find that they had sheltered very near the clump of trees where Reinhardt had nursed Sebastian back to health.

"Do you suppose the horse remembered this spot?" Johann asked, shivering in his damp clothes.

"I don't know."

Reinhardt was quiet and thoughtful.

"Well, in any case, now we know the way back to town so perhaps we should return ...."

"If you don't mind," Reinhardt interrupted, "I should like to go back to that fork in the road where Old Swift bolted. You know the place where she stopped before she took off at such high speed."

Johann sighed dolefully as he climbed back onto the wagon.

"I don't know why you're asking me. You're going to do it anyway. Well, come on then. Harness the creature and lets hope she stays calm this morning."

Reinhardt smiled. Old Swift nuzzled his neck as he harnessed her, a picture of sweetness and tranquility.

Almost one-half hour later, picking their way through lake-sized mud-puddles, they were back at the junction where they had lost their bearings the night before. The divide lay open, with no apparent obstruction. Reinhardt halted the wagon and rested his chin on his hands.

"It is a mystery to me," he said, "why God would not have had us go towards the farm-house."

"God?" Johann responded, "It was your horse, Reinhardt. She was startled by something – something we have not discovered yet and perhaps never shall."

"Well," Reinhardt said, "never in all the time I have had her has she ever disobeyed a command. So why she should do so now is a ...."

"Well, she did disobey," Johann interrupted, "I can certainly attest to that. Now let's turn the wagon and get back on track. Now I don't intend that we should travel back to town, but propose we head over to your farm. I daresay your mother and sister are very worried and I would not put it beyond them to start for town on foot to make sure that you are well."

Reinhardt smiled.

"Yes, they would be capable of doing that," he answered, straightway clucking and pulling at the reins.

Old Swift obeyed him immediately, setting off down the path she had rejected so violently the previous evening.

They had not traveled longer than a few minutes through the storm-water runoff road when Reinhardt suddenly tugged hard on the reins.

"Look," he whispered to Johann.

Sebastian, who had been looking up at the forest around them, awed at the beauty of the wet leaves and the soft dripping of water onto the undergrowth, was startled out of his reverie.

"What?"

And then he saw what Reinhardt saw. Not too far ahead, at the right side of the road, a man was struggling to sit upright. Half-concealed by the brush, half out in the open, he appeared to be tangled up in ropes.

Johann peering hard and appearing to recognize the fellow, straight away called out, "Hendrick! Hendrick! Is that you?!"

The man thrashed about, tried to speak, but could only croak hoarsely in reply. Reinhardt urged Old Swift on, and the horse trotted towards the place where the man half-sat and half-lay. Johann was off the wagon in an instant and at the man's side.

"Hendrick! Hendrick! What happened to you, man?"

Hendrick's eyes were glazed and he smiled weakly, unable to speak.

"Reinhardt, give me your water flask."

Reinhardt took the flask from his waist-belt and handed it over it to Johann. Johann knelt down by Hendrick, cradled his head in his arms and trickled some water into the man's mouth.

"Alive," Hendrick muttered, as soon as he had swallowed a few mouthfuls, "you are alive."

"Of course I am alive, you dolt! Why shouldn't I be alive?"

"Gunther," Hendrick said.

"Reinhardt, do you have your knife handy? We've got to cut these ropes off Hendrick's hands and legs."

Reinhardt again obliged and Johann proceeded to free Hendrick from the firmly bound cords that held him captive.

"Who did this to you?"

"Gunther," the reply was a little stronger this time.

Johann rubbed Hendrick's numbed hands and legs, all the while muttering angrily.

"Well, where is Gunther?" Reinhardt asked, looking down the road to where it curved sharply to the right.

Hendrick pointed to where Reinhardt had been looking and spoke again.

"Gunther was worried."

He got the words out with some difficulty.

"Why was he worried?" Reinhardt asked.

"The men he hired to beat you ... they did not return last night. He thought they might have ...."

"Might have what?"

Johann was impatient.

"That they might have fallen asleep or ... that they might have decided to ... tell the authorities ...."

The words had totally worn him out. He closed his eyes. Together Johann and Reinhardt lifted Hendrick into the back of the wagon. Then they climbed back onto the front themselves.

"We should get him to mother and Elza," Reinhardt said as soon as Old Swift began to move again, "I vow that Gunther and his cronies will be far gone by now. Later we can report the incident to the town authorities."

"He kept calling," Hendrick suddenly spoke quite clearly from the back of the wagon. "He just kept calling."

"What did he keep calling?" Sebastian asked, half-turning to face Hendrick.

"That he was not you and that he was not the Jew."

Reinhardt and Johann eyed each other. The wagon now turned the corner. Old Swift stopped in her tracks. Someone lay on the left side of the road. Obviously pummeled and beaten black and blue, the dead body of Gunther greeted them.

And though the world with devils filled,
Should threaten to undo us,
We will not fear, for God has willed
His truth to triumph through us.
The prince of darkness grim,
We tremble not for him;
His rage we can endure,
For Lo! His doom is sure,
One little word shall fell him.

The providence of God is a strange and wonderful thing. Every blade of grass, every rain drop, every flash of lightning, is under God's command. And so is death, life and the pattern of a horse's steps.

Lena in the Hand

For I the LORD love justice;
I hate robbery and wrong;
I will faithfully give them their recompense,
and I will make an everlasting covenant with them.
Their offspring shall be known among the nations,
and their descendants in the midst of the peoples;
all who see them shall acknowledge them,
that they are an offspring the LORD has blessed.
I will greatly rejoice in the LORD;
my soul shall exult in my God,
for he has clothed me with the garments of salvation;
he has covered me with the robe of righteousness,
as a bridegroom decks himself like a priest with a beautiful
headdress, and as a bride adorns herself with her jewels.
For as the earth brings forth its sprouts,
and as a garden causes what is sown in it to sprout up,
so the Lord GOD will cause righteousness and praise
to sprout up before all the nations (Is. 61:-11).

The moment they were close to the city gates, Agatha took her young companion by the hand. It was early morning but not so early that the Strasbourg birds had not already begun to sing. Lena, for that was the girl's name, frequently lifted her eyes skyward, stumbling on her brown shoes as she did so, trying to make out where these birds were that sang so beautifully. It earned her a sharp tug. Agatha was in a hurry, but even in her hurry she took the time to glance over her shoulder every few minutes, all the while muttering under her breath.

"Come, Lena. Do not dawdle. If that is the way you begin your new life, you will not do well. No, you will not do well at all."

"Will you miss me, Agatha?"

The words were plaintive, but there was no answer. Lena had not expected any. Agatha, although well-meaning, rarely answered queries. Caught however, somewhere between childhood and womanhood, Lena needed assurance. She harbored a mixture of emotions which made her feel somewhat shivery inside. Consequently, she asked once more.

"Agatha, will you miss me?"

Again there was no answer for the pair had now arrived at the Cronenbourg Gate on the west side of Strasbourg and Agatha had to stand still for a moment to assess where exactly they were. Lena knew where they were. She knew in a bittersweet way. In the past she had frequently walked through the Cronenbourg gate with her father. Swallowing audibly at the memory, she again tripped slightly as Agatha, having gotten her bearings, suddenly renewed her walk. Lena's gangly frame dismally traipsed alongside that of Agatha's tall bulk. Her father's voice accompanied them.

"Lena," he said, "let's stop and see if we can spot some birds."

"Oh, yes, father," she replied softly under her breath.

Recalling the wonderful times that they had actually done so, she smiled. On the not-so-distant past horizon, she glimpsed a middle-aged man and his teenaged daughter abandoning with child-like glee a cart with etchings by the side of the road; she caught sight of them stretching flat on their backs in the lush grass contemplating the glorious blue sky; and she remembered them making out faces in the clouds as they listened to the choir of birds singing their hearts out in the trees and in the meadow. Agatha tugged her hand again.

"What ails you, Lena? Don't day-dream. Walk faster. We're supposed to be at the beguinage before long."

"Yes, Agatha."

"Always mind what the Meisterin says to you. Always obey what she wants you to do, Lena. And when you get used to your surroundings, try to do things before she, or any of the sister beguines, asks you."

"Yes, Agatha."

"And be polite."

"Yes, Agatha."

"Compared to Hagenau, folks in Strasbourg are a mite more ...."

Lena did not hear what Agatha's comments about the folks in Strasbourg were for she had begun feasting her eyes on the wide scope of Strasbourg's skyline - a skyline dominated by church spires. Looking straight up as they passed through the silent streets, she beheld houses and more houses. The gables, with their numerous attic windows, ran straight into the clouds. They were all richly engrafted with wreathed work, stone carvings, left-overs of previous centuries. Agatha pulled her hand. They were now walking straight across an old suburb called Stone Street, and heading towards Bishop's Castle Gate. There must be a great many people, Lena surmised, who lived in these beautiful, stone houses. Perhaps girls just like herself often walked here with their friends on their way to the market. Or perhaps boys strode by on their way to work at the Horse Market, or a smithy, or.... As if from very far away, she heard her Agatha's voice drone on and on with admonitions, and she kept nodding and saying 'Yes, Agatha'. On her right and very high, she espied the church spire of the Cathedral. She and father had often walked up to the Cathedral just because it was tremendous and made them feel so very small.

"God," father had said, "lives here, Lena."

"God, father? But I thought He lived in heaven?"

"He does, child. He does. But He also has a place here."

"Are you sure? I thought the priests lived in church."

He had nodded.

"They have surely tried to supplant Him. But God is everywhere, child."

Unlike the houses, the church had no gables. It was just high, very high. God was high. Was He too high for her to reach? When she was very little she had asked her father if God rang the bells in the Cathedral. She smiled now to think of it.

"Perhaps He does ring these bells, Lena. He surely calls people. I know that He calls them," her father had answered, "just as I know that the Ammeister, the mayor, might call people to meetings."

Father had known a lot about God. He had often listened to the traveling priests who preached the new doctrine. Father had tried to translate the new doctrine into plain words for her. If you believe, he had told her, then God has chosen you. When she had asked him what it meant to be chosen, he had explained that it was as if God picked you up and held you in His hand. But he had told her this just before he had died, just before Agatha had folded father's hands on his chest and just before they had taken him away to be buried. Now she could not ask him any more. Lena stared up at the Cathedral again as they passed. It was magnificent! Would the beguines take her inside this church? Would she be able to climb its two towers? She peered thoughtfully at the single spire - a spire known to be the tallest in all of Europe. Strasbourg was a good city to live in this year of our Lord, 1529. So Agatha had told her again and again this past week. Yet, she felt tears sting behind her eyelids. It had been a good city when she had come here with father those times when he had conducted business with various printers. It had been a good city because father had loved her and had been there with her. She furtively glanced sideways at Agatha. Agatha was a large woman - a midwife who knew a great many things about herbs and about birthing. Highly respected in Hagenau, she had always been a good friend to father and herself. They had boarded in her house for a great many years. Agatha was capable and strong. Lena's thin hand and wrist fairly disappeared within her grasp. And Agatha truly did love her. She knew that. Once when she had wept because Agatha had punished her for daydreaming, father had told her that Agatha was a practical person; a person who was somehow unable to stop and look at the uniqueness of things. Agatha saw, for example, father explained, the need to have onions for soup but she was not one who was able to sit back and contemplate the beauty of the vegetable; she was not moved to feel the silky softness of the onion skin and to stroke its green ears. Lena grinned to herself. Ears indeed! Onion ears! How could father have said such a thing? Or when Agatha sees a rabbit, father had continued, she immediately sees it stewing in the pot. She cannot be bothered to take the time to watch it hop, to be amazed at the twitching of its whiskers and the quivering of its little nose. Often at dusk Lena had sat with father and had watched rabbits. Agatha thought it a waste of time and....

"Lena, child, where are your thoughts. Here is the beguinage."

They had entered a courtyard, a courtyard surrounded by a stone gate and harboring several small buildings. Secluded from Strassbourg proper by this gate through which they had just passed, it lay quietly and peacefully in the spring sunshine. Lena could feel the stillness as if it were a garment someone had just wrapped around her.

"Now, child," Agatha said, and stopped, as if she was about to say more.

Lena looked up at her, surprised. Agatha rarely addressed her as child - always she said Lena.

"Yes, Agatha."

Agatha's hand pulled her over to a bench under a tree in the center of the courtyard.

"I want to speak with you before you go in, before the time that I might not be able to see... that is to say, to speak with you privately as I do now."

"Yes, Agatha."

They sat down and Agatha's hands began straightening Lena's hair, hair which perpetually escaped from under her small white cap.

"You must, of course, mind what the Meisterin says," Agatha repeated for the hundredth time, but then she went on, even as her right hand continued to stroke Lena's forehead, "and I want you to be careful, Lena. Very careful."

"Careful?" Lena repeated, lifting large, blue eyes to stare at Agatha's face.

"Yes," Agatha said, "there are many people in the world who cannot be trusted. Mind you, I will try to visit you from time to time. For surely I promised your father I would look after you. But you are not my lawful ward. I would keep you in Hagenau with me, Lena, but I am so busy and am often gone to deliver newborn babies and ...."

"I know, Agatha," Lena softly said, "and I am so grateful that you have helped me even when there was no one else except cousin Jurgen, mother's cousin, and he, of course, cannot take care of me, because he is a priest."

"Yes," Agatha answered, a trifle loudly, "cousin Jurgen. And this is what I want to say to you, Lena. Cousin Jurgen will likely come to visit some time in the future. Now I know it is as you say, he is a distant cousin of your mother, God rest her soul, but I fear he does not always have your best interest at heart."

Lena did not remember her mother who had died when she was born. And she had only met cousin Jurgen once or twice when he had come to call on father. Father had not liked him, she recalled, and had made fun of him.

"He's a trickster, Lena," he had said, "all well-wishes with his right hand, while he is looking to see what he can take from you with his left."

She nodded at Agatha.

"I will be careful," she promised.

"There is something else," Agatha went on, reaching into one of the deep pockets of her kirtle, "This, child, is yours."

Lena stared at a little cloth bag, tied at the top with a small, blue ribbon.

"What is it, Agatha?"

"It is money, child," Agatha whispered in a low-pitched voice, "money your father entrusted to me before he died of the plague, God rest his soul. It is for you, child. Since the day of your birth, he regularly set aside some money whenever he sold some of his etchings. He instructed me to keep it for you for a dowry. He said that if he did not give it to me, his creditors would eat it up. Now this is what I want to say to you. Somehow your cousin Jurgen has gotten the smell of your father's money, your money, in his nostrils and he sent word to me that he wants to discuss placing you in a convent. He says that since he is a blood relative, he has the authority to do so."

"A convent?"

"Yes."

Agatha left off speaking. There was no noise in the courtyard but the quiet buzzing of a bee lazily flying about some flowers at their feet.

"I do not want to go into a convent," Lena said slowly, by and by, as she stared at the bushes and the flowers surrounding them, "I did not even want to go here, but I know you cannot keep me always as I am not your own daughter."

Agatha smiled and patted Lena's hand.

"Besides," Lena went on, "father said that he was prone to the new faith, the faith that is being preached here in Strasbourg and also in Hagenau. You know that he was. He said this faith was plainer than what the priests taught, and before he died, he told me I was to listen to the new preachers should I have opportunity, even as he did."

"I know, child," Agatha said, patting Lena's hand, "But here, in this beguinage, I do believe you will presently be safer than with me in Hagenau. And I think you shall have more freedom than ever you would in a convent. Women live here in harmony. They try to serve God in various activities. Best of all, you are free to leave, if you should so desire. It is a good place for you at this moment in time, Lena, for when cousin Jurgen comes to see me, as I am sure he shall, I will be able to say you are happily settled in a beguinage. Despite his blood relationship to you, he will not be able to move you quickly from this place to a convent.

Lena nodded, not truly understanding Agatha's words.

Here," Agatha went on, putting the cloth bag into Lena's hand, closing the girl's fingers over it, "there are some fifty gold coins in it. You must hide this carefully as soon as you are settled in a room somewhere and you ought to tell no one, no one at all, that you have it."

"What about the fee the beguinage requires so that I might stay here?"

"Yes, yes," Agatha said, "that is taken care of. Don't fret about it. And now," she continued, "we must go in or the Meisterin will be thinking we fell into a well, or that robbers attacked us."

Lena laughed, for she rarely heard Agatha joke and surely this was a joke.

"Remember," Agatha repeated, falling back into her admonishings, standing up and taking hold of Lena's hand again, "do what the Meisterin says."

"Yes, Agatha," she dutifully answered, even as she inserted the cloth bag deep within the confines of her kirtle's pocket with her other hand, "I will."

They walked towards the main building, halting before the beguinage door. Agatha lifted her hand to ring the bronze bell hanging on the wall next to the door. But before she did so, she glanced over her shoulder to see if anyone was behind them, if anyone was watching them over the stone wall protecting the courtyard from the street. Satisfied there was no one, she turned back towards the heavy bronze bell. Her capable hand rang loudly. Even though the sound reverberated there was no immediate answer. A few minutes elapsed. Lena looked around. The courtyard was large. Even as she was staring, her eyes seemed to catch the face of someone peering at them from behind the stone wall. It was at that moment that Agatha let go of her hand and began banging on the oak door with both of her fists. Startled, Lena turned her face back to the door.

"They will hear that!" Agatha commented, "And perhaps they will pay more attention to such a noise than that bell. There is no need to keep us waiting, walk as we did so early."

Even as she spoke there was a commotion behind the door.

"Yes, yes, do you want to waken the dead? I heard you. I heard you."

The door was unlatched, and the face of an older woman peered through a crack.

"I am Agatha Lichtenberg come to bring my charge Lena to the Meisterin of Gotteshaus zum Wolf as a novice beguine."

"Ah," the woman breathed.

The great door opened wider and revealed a hall, a hall spotless and shiny with tiles arranged in rows and rows of square clouds. Square clouds? Father would laugh at her if she told him this. Clouds are not square, child, he would have said, they are round. The thought made Lena gentle with love, until she remembered that father was gone and noted that the woman was scrutinizing her carefully. Unconsciously her hands slid down to smooth the dark blue kirtle Agatha had bought her for the funeral. She could feel the small cloth bag deep down in her pocket. Then she blushed and concentrated on her brown shoes.

"Meisterin asked that you be shown to her quarters when you arrived. Please follow me."

Hard on the portress' heels, they walked through the long hall, at length turning into one of the many rooms on the left. It was a bright and cheery room. There was a wonderfully spacious window facing the east and the light of the morning sun fell through it with great splendor. A woman rose from a chair and offered an outstretched hand which Agatha took.

"You must be Agatha Lichtenberg," and a smile accompanied the words, "I'm glad that you were able to travel safely to our home. And you," the smile now turned to Lena, "must be the young Lena whom we are to have the pleasure of housing here in Gotteshaus zum Wolf."

Lena nodded, dumb with shyness, and curtsied at the same time. She eyed the Meisterin with obvious admiration. Her gown was a rich brown color. But the rich brown was not what made the gown so attractive. It was the gold crucifix. Off-setting the chocolate brown, glittering and dangling from her waist, it reached half-way down to the floor and gave Meisterin a serene and capable aura.

"I'm happy to meet you, young Lena."

The voice was soft and yet it was by no means weak. It was a voice which knew what it wanted; a voice that would not be brooked.

"I am happy to make your acquaintance also, Meisterin," Lena answered softly.

She curtsied again, not because manners dictated that she do so, but because she felt she must do something to indicate that she was impressed with the room, with Meisterin and with the brightness of the window.

"Welcome, Lena," Meisterin answered her "Indeed, welcome and I hope very much that you will feel at home here."

"She is used to hard labor."

Agatha, who had stood surveying the room as well, interposed in a rather sharp voice, a voice that reminded Lena she was not to trust people too readily.

"You will," Meisterin responded to Agatha in a steady voice, "very much miss your charge, Agatha. You will surely feel the loss of her company in the days to come."

It was a statement, not a question. Lena pondered it quietly as she stood looking down at her shoes without moving. She did not think it likely that Agatha would yearn for her. She would be too busy with her own work. Many expecting mothers in Hagenau depended on Agatha. Agatha loved her work. Indeed, she had taught many of the skills of midwifery to Lena as well.

"Lena."

It was Agatha's voice. Startled, she looked up.

"Meisterin is speaking to you."

Shifting her gaze away from Agatha, Lena's apologetic gaze met the half-smile of Meisterin.

"I beg your pardon," she stuttered, curtsying again out of sheer embarrassment.

"I asked if you were hungry after your long walk?"

"No... that is, yes."

"Well, just go down to the kitchen and cook will give you some bread and ale."

Lena looked at her Agatha, who nodded slightly. Then she turned and walked towards the door through which they had just entered. Resting her hand on the wooden handle, she hesitated, turning about again.

"It's fine, child," Meisterin assured her, "just turn left. The kitchen is at the end of the hall. Tell cook I sent you."

****

It took Lena a few weeks to settle in. Her main jobs were scrubbing the hall, helping cook in the kitchen and being sent on errands. She gradually began to know some of the other women. At regular times each day she ate with and had devotions with all the other members of the sisterhood. These devotions consisted of reading tales of martyrs, women and men who had died for their faith, and these devotions could be rather graphic. Lena had been assigned a room with a much older woman, a Gertrude Rosslin. Sister Gertrude, as she was asked to call her, was garrulous, snored and manifested an unhealthy interest in Lena's background. Mostly bed-ridden, she rarely left the confines of the room.

"Where are you from, child?"

"Hagenau, sister Gertrude."

"Why are you here? You are still almost a child? No young suitor?"

Lena blushed.

"No, sister Gertrude."

"Where are your parents, child?"

"They are dead, sister Gertrude."

"Who paid your entry fee into Gotteshaus zum Wolf?"

This was a difficult question, a question Lena also often asked herself. Like as not, Agatha had paid it, perhaps from some of the gold coins in the little linen bag. Lena slept with the linen bag tied to her undergarments.

"Child, I asked you a question."

"I don't know, sister Gertrude."

"Did no one ever tell you that lying is a wicked sin, child? It will earn you years and years in purgatory."

"But I truly don't know the answer to your question, sister Gertrude."

"My father paid for my fee. Though I should be free to marry, he said, should a proposal come my way, should a good man wish to make me his spouse."

"Perhaps," Lena opted, smiling at the older woman who had wisps of grey escaping her cream cap, "a good man will still come and want to marry you. I should not be surprised."

She knew in her heart that this truly was a lie. But sister Gertrude seemed not to note. Truth be told, sister Gertrude was not handsome. There was a wart on her chin and she had the misfortune to be slightly cross-eyed. Neither was she easy to live with. She constantly ordered Lena, and whoever else was about, to do things for her.

"See if cook has a sweetmeat, child", "Bring me a drink a water," and "Have the goodness to rinse that stain out of my pillow", and phrases like it were repeated over and over. It took much forbearance on Lena's part to be kind to the older woman. But she knew that the older woman was much alone.

A week after her arrival at Gotteshaus zum Wolf, sister Gertrude caught Lena carefully studying the room they shared. She was trying to ascertain whether or not there might be a hiding place somewhere - a small spot where she might stash away her little bag so that she might not have to carry it all the time.

"What are you looking for, child?"

Sister Gertrude had eyes like a hawk and from her corner chair it seemed that she ruled the room.

"I know that you are looking for something," she persisted when Lena did not answer. "Come, come, child, we are roommates and roommates help one another. You have been absent-minded most of the afternoon. I noted it well. Why don't you tell me what is bothering you."

The words were comforting, seemingly kindhearted. Before she knew it, Lena had confided in sister Gertrude the how and why of her need for a secret place. At the end of her story, the older woman's rheumy eyes were closed and Lena thought she might have fallen asleep. But then she spoke.

"I know where you might hide your money in this room, Lena. It is a good place and well-camouflaged. I'm the only one who knows about it and no one will ever find it."

"Where is it?"

Slowly and painfully, sister Gertrude got up from her chair and walked over to the bricked wall, the wall opposite from where she had been sitting. Counting ten layers upward from the floor and twenty sideways from the door, she fingered one of the bricks. Pushing it sideways, it gave way, revealing a small niche. A green cloth bag stood in the niche, presumably holding sister Gertrude's valuables.

"It is my special hiding place," sister Gertrude said rather proudly, "and I have had it for these past twenty years without anyone ever finding it."

"Oh," Lena replied, moving to stand next to sister Gertrude.

She noted that the space was big enough to also contain her linen bag.

"Well," sister Gertrude barked, "go ahead. Put your money next to mine."

"You will not," Lena began a trifle nervously, "ever tell anyone, or take any ...."

She stopped. Perhaps asking someone if they would steal your money was not the proper way to say things. Perhaps suggesting such a thing might just trigger some dishonesty within a heart.

"Take any of your money?" sister Gertrude responded in a rather loud and very offended voice, "What are you saying, Lena? I have just shown you where my money is and you think that I would...?"

She stopped and retraced her steps back to her chair where she sat down, her wart quivering with indignation. Lena felt ashamed.

"No, of course you wouldn't."

"Well, then, go ahead, put your money next to mine and then please go and get some oil from the dispensary to rub onto my sore leg."

Lena complied. But later in bed, she worried that she ought to have kept the bag on her person. Now she had two people to worry about - sister Gertrude and cousin Jurgen.

The third week that Lena came to reside in Gotteshaus zum Wolf, the Meisterin summoned her and asked if she might enjoy helping to care for a child whose mother was a little weary and who was shortly to have another baby. It seemed to Lena that to leave the confines of the beguinage and the constant grumbling of sister Gertrude, although she was becoming genuinely fond of the old lady, would be wonderful.

"Oh, yes, Meisterin," she breathed, "I would be happy to help."

"Agatha informed me that you had skill in caring for children, and that she had instructed you in helping to care for newborns."

"Yes."

Lena drew in her breath as she spoke, eagerly waiting for what Meisterin would tell her.

"Our beguinage is often asked to aid families in the community. But the money earned will be given to us, you understand."

The words cavorted around in Lena's head, but she scarcely heard them. She could only think of the new freedom coming her way. She had been so used to roaming about with her father, to accompanying Agatha on calls, that the beguinage was becoming stifling. This seemed heavensent.

"There is something else, Lena."

"Yes, Meisterin."

"A brother Jurgen, a cousin, he said of your mother, called here last week. Perhaps I should have spoken to you earlier. It was just at the time that you were running an errand for sister Gertrude - a rather lengthy errand. So I could not call you to meet with him. He was rather insistent that he see you and said something about you having some money that should be entrusted to him?"

Lena did not reply. She did not know what to say. Truthfully, she would never entrust any money to cousin Jurgen. Perhaps she ought to take the linen bag out of the hiding place and begin carrying it on her person again.

Meisterin was watching her closely. She felt her cheeks getting red.

"What should I tell Brother Jurgen if he should call again, Lena?"

"That I have no money for him," Lena forced out of a dry throat. "but, yes, he is a distant cousin."

"Well, if he is a relative, there is no harm in a visit, is there? I'm sure the misunderstanding about the money can be cleared up. He seemed a pleasant enough priest. Apparently, he was recently placed in Strasbourg and has already enjoyed a visit with sister Gertrude. Did she not mention it to you?"

"No, Meisterin."

"Well, no matter. Here is the address to which you will betake yourself tomorrow. May God bless your work in that household."

The interview ended on that note.

The next morning, after communal devotions, Lena left the beguinage courtyard and contentedly strolled through several streets north of the beguinage towards the Gertner home eager to begin to help care for little Bernhard Gertner. Herr Gertner, his father, was a merchant and often gone from home. Bernhard was a healthy boy, safe for the fact that he had a deformity, a stiffness in his neck. Frau Gertner, heavy with her next child, informed Lena that the deformity was the result of having been swaddled wrongly by the midwife after he was born. The doctor had recently prescribed a new salve which Lena was to rub on the child's neck early each morning when she arrived at the Gertner home. Consequently, every day Lena patiently rubbed the cream on the boy's small neck from the crucible in which it came, all the while talking to Bernhard, telling him stories - stories which she had heard from her father when she was a little maid.

Weeks passed peaceably. Cousin Jurgen did not return to Gotteshaus Zum Wolf. Lena began to relax. She enjoyed taking care of Bernhard and Margarethe Gertner, Bernhard's mother, grew very fond of Lena. Because Bernhard was six, he had begun formal education and attended a Latin school. Every half past nine, with the exception of Sunday, after the salve was rubbed on, Lena and Bernhard set off from the Gertner home to walk the several blocks down to the Lehrmeister's home.

"I have to learn to write well," Bernhard confided in Lena, as he held her hand and skipped along, "so that I can help father when I am bigger."

She nodded gravely.

"Where is your father, Lena?"

He had asked this question before, but she had never answered him.

"He is dead," she now answered suddenly, even as a horse-drawn carriage passed by on the street. Some pedestrians loitered about shops, and the occasional beggar sat by the curb. Beggars were actually not allowed in Strasbourg. But what, Lena thought, if you had nothing at all.

"What is dead, Lena?"

She stopped walking and stood still. The church spire of the Cathedral overshadowed them.

"What is dead, Lena?"

The little boy persisted in his question, looking up at her with his neck at an awkward angle.

"Does dead mean you can't play with your father anymore? I know that our cook had a cat that died. It got really stiff and couldn't move and then...."

"Hush," Lena answered, beginning to stride forward once more but at a quicker pace, and pulling the child along rather too fast for Bernhard's liking.

"Why are you cross, Lena?"

Twisting his face up again, the child perceived that tears were running down Lena's face, and not being able to conceive of any sorrow that could not be fixed by a kiss, he stopped so quickly that his hand slid out of hers. She stopped also, wiping her cheeks with the back of her hand.

"Don't disobey, Bernhard."

The words came out rather muffled.

"I'm not disobeying," the boy said, and then stepping close to her, he flung his arms around her waist, continuing, "don't worry, Lena, I won't die. I don't even know how to die."

"Dead," said Lena, "dead is gone... dead is not there...."

She halted and the tears began again. Bernhard pulled her over to the church steps. They were standing right by the cathedral and it seemed very logical to the child that the steps be used for sitting.

"I heard Mutti talking about dying. She said that when the new baby comes, she might die."

He leaned heavily against Lena, his small arm about her waist.

"You might be late for school, Bernhard, if we keep talking and not walking."

"Mutti," the boy continued, not paying any heed, "has an eagle stone to help her stay healthy while she is carrying the baby. It is a hollow, round stone and has a rock inside it that rattles when you shake it. She wears it round her neck on a gold chain and the baby can hear it."

He looked up at her with a smile, again painfully twisting his neck as he did so.

"Mutti wore the same stone when I was in her belly. It strengthened me, as you can see."

Lena could not help but smile down at him.

"Yes, you are a strong boy."

"Well, except for my stiff neck maybe. And when it is time for the baby to be born, the stone will be tied to Mutti's right knee. It is called an eagle stone, Lena, because it fell down from an eagle in the sky."

She nodded and he was relieved to see that her tears had stopped. She smiled again, but that smile suddenly froze on her face, and her features contorted with fear.

"What is it, Lena?"

Bernhard carefully turned his head towards the space where she was gazing. But he saw nothing unusual.

"It is of no matter," the girl replied.

"Yes," Bernhard persisted, "I know you saw something that scared you."

"Well," Lena admitted nervously, "I thought I saw my cousin, a brother Jurgen, standing in the street looking at me. He ...."

She broke off speaking and half stood up. Bernhard's arm fell down, and she reached for it and pulled him up as well.

"He is a priest, and I have only seen him a few times, so I can't be sure."

"Let's go into the church," Bernhard suggested, shaking loose his arm and walking backwards up the steps as he scanned the street, "No-one can hurt you in the cathedral. Besides that, Pastor Zell might be there."

"Pastor Zell? Who is he?"

Lena cautiously followed the boy up the stairs.

"He is my friend, and he is teaching me catechism."

Lena let herself be guided along up the church steps. Casting backward glances at the street, she was anxious and her body was stiff with apprehension. What if cousin Jurgen was here? Was he searching for her? Reaching the top of the stairs, Bernhard opened the great cathedral doors. Lena followed him into the massive building. The door fell shut behind them and the echo of its closing reverberated with a cavernous sound throughout. the foyer in which they were standing. The hollow noise frightened her and instinctively she reached for Bernhard's hand.

"It's all right, Lena," he whispered.

Hand in hand, they warily walked into the sanctuary. A scattering of people was seated in the benches, praying, heads down. Without thinking, Lena began walking on her tip toes. Exquisite stained-glass windows on both sides of the sanctuary were awesome and matchless. Holding her breath, Lena continued with Bernhard towards the front of the church, turning right into a small narthex.

"This is the chapel of Saint Lorenz, " Bernhard whispered, "and that", he added, pointing to a wooden dais at the front, "is Pastor Zell's pulpit. Some people did not, you see," he explained in a voice wise beyond his years, "want him preaching from the big pulpit in the main cathedral."

"Why not?" Lena automatically asked, even though she did not know Pastor Zell, nor who it was whose pulpit he was not allowed to use.

"Because ...," Bernhard began, but cut his sentence short when he noted a man approaching them.

"Hello, Bernhard," the man said, "it is not Thursday, you know. Did you forget? Pastor Zell did preach earlier but he is not in presently."

"I thought he might be in, but that is all right," Bernhard replied.

"And who is your friend?"

The man, possibly in his mid-twenties, had a kind face with sympathetic, warm eyes. He very much reminded Lena of her father.

"This is Lena. She takes me to school every day and picks me up afterwards and walks me home."

"Hello, Lena."

Because the girl seemed shy and did not reply, the man continued.

"My name is Paul Josselin. I am one of the carpenters who dissembles and moves Pastor Zell's portable pulpit each time he preaches and I am surely honored to meet Bernhard's friend and keeper. He surely needs a keeper."

Lena smiled and blushed at the same time but still said nothing in reply.

"Lena thought she saw a man outside who ...."

Bernhard did not get any further. Lena's hand shot out and covered his mouth.

"Hush, Bernhard!"

"Was someone bothering you?" the carpenter asked.

"She thought," Bernhard went on undeterred, as he pulled Lena's hand away from his mouth, "that this priest...."

"Priest?"

"Yes, that is what Lena said, she called him Brother Jurgen."

Again Lena's hand shot out. Again she tried to cover Bernhard's mouth in another attempt to maintain her privacy.

"You must hush your talk, Bernhard!"

"But Herr Josselin is strong and he will protect you. Won't you, Herr Josselin?"

After these words, Bernhard grinned at Paul Josselin, who smiled back but at the same time motioned that Lena should sit down on one of the pews behind her and rest. Hesitantly, she took a step back and sat down.

"Please forgive my intrusion," he spoke softly as he sat down next to her, "but be assured that I only mean to help you if you face some sort of difficulty. I am well acquainted with the Gertner family who will vouch for me. You need not hesitate to trust me."

Lena blushed again, and the redness of her cheeks well became her. Paul Josselin noted it and wondered greatly how such a seemingly refined and gentle girl came to be in the company of Bernhard who had sat down on his other side. He ruffled the boy's hair.

"Were you working on the pulpit, Herr Josselin?"

"I was indeed. I just waiting for Martin Schutzer to help me store it away until the next time."

Paul Josselin continued studying Lena's face as he spoke. The girl was staring at the floor. She seemed afraid of something and he instinctively felt a need to protect her.

Content to miss school, Bernhard stood up and faced the couple. Turning around, he wedged his small form between Lena and Paul.

Leaning against Lena, he whispered to her, "I told you that it would be good to come in here."

"I'm not sure what your mother will say when she hears you missed part of your lessons," Lena whispered back, but she did not stir from her spot.

"If you wait, I will conduct you safely to the Lehrmeister's house."

Lena nodded agreement to Paul Josselin. She instinctively felt he could be trusted and surely, anyone who was welcome in the Gertner home was a good person'

"And remember," Herr Josselin continued, as he rose and walked towards the pulpit, "in the long run you are not in my hands, but in the hands of God our Father. And no one can harm you there."

Lena studied her right hand. It was a small hand, to be sure, but callouses had formed on the fingers from her routinely scrubbing the beguinage hallway. How peculiar it was to think of a person being in a hand. What a strange way to phrase something.

"If you wait a few minutes, I shall be ready."

Beginning the dismantling of the pulpit, Paul Josslin uttered the words reassuringly, and Lena nodded again.

On the way to the Lehrmeister's home in order to set his charge at ease, Paul Josselin continued to speak kindly. An able guide, he pointed out various homes and landmarks as they walked, noting with pleasure that she appreciated his help and knowledge. She had just begun to softly question him about Pastor Zell when someone touched her shoulder from behind.

"Hello, cousin Lena."

The voice was spindly and lean, but she heard the words as if they had been shouted from one of the rooftops in the gabled street. Turning ever so slightly, she felt repugnance at the profile she had been dreading. It was silhouetted against the side wall. She answered not a word but stiffened perceptibly. Bernhard felt it instantly and twisted his crooked neck to stare up at her. Lena had clenched her hands into fists and she shivered. Painfully Bernhard turned his head further and saw the priest, as did Paul Josselin.

"Lena," whispered Bernhard, "is that the man you are afraid of?"

Brother Jurgen as well heard the child's words clearly.

"Afraid of me?" he said much louder than his greeting had been, "Afraid of her own mother's cousin? That is ridiculous!"

Paul Josselin stopped and turned to face the priest.

"Hello," he said agreeably, "did you wish to speak with this young woman?"

"She is my cousin," Brother Jurgen answered stiffly, "and who might you be, sir?"

Paul Josselin did not answer, but contemplated Lena. Her hands, still clenched into fists, regarded the priest with a mixture of distaste and revulsion.

"Why," asked the girl, "is it that you follow me and say that I must entrust you with my money? And," she added emphatically, "I do not want to be placed in a convent."

"A convent?" Paul Josselin interjected.

"You, nameless sir," the priest rejoined, "have nothing to do with this conversation at all. So kindly hold your tongue!"

Bernhard had taken one of Lena's hands, and undoing the fist, had clasped her fingers within his own. Paul noted this out of the corner of his eye and he patted the boy on his head. Lena was very pale now and her voice trembled as she spoke.

"My father had no liking for you, cousin Jurgen, and I am quite well settled in the beguinage."

"Yes, I know this. The truth is that I have visited your roommate, sister Gertrude, to make certain that you are... that you are well cared for and well situated."

He hesitated and then continued.

"Sister Gertrude has assured me that you are doing well. Yes, she told me...," he stopped and eyed her in a proprietorial way," she told me many things."

Lena became even paler. Paul Josselin moved closer to her.

"I think we might continue walking," he said in a low voice to the girl, "and you can rest assured that I shall not leave you unprotected."

She smiled at him.

"Thank you, Paul."

Unconsciously and with ease she called him by his first name and this pleased him greatly. They turned away from Brother Jurgen, but as they continued down the street, the priest called after them.

"You are my ward, you know, Lena. This I can prove as your mother was my second cousin. And Agatha Lichtenberg, who placed you in the beguinage, is only an acquaintance."

Lena shivered again. Bernhard and Paul flanked her, each one walking on either side. A few moments later, Bernhard painfully grinned up at Lena.

"That was exciting. I much prefer that to reciting Latin phrases."

Both Lena and Paul smiled.

"I think," Lena ventured, "that we should return to the Gertner home, for it is by this time almost the hour at which Bernhard is usually finished with his lessons."

The summer months passed and, as they passed, it came to be that Lena began to be included in many of the Gertner family activities. Invited to attend church with them, she heard both Pastor Zell and Paston Firn, his colleague, preach on a regular basis. Her small knowledge of the Scriptures increased, as did her desire to know more. She also regularly saw Paul Josselin. A frequent visitor to the Gertner household, he was much loved by the entire family. Taking a keen interest in Lena, he encouraged her in all manner of things. She and Bernhard frequently visited his workshop, admired his wood carvings and furniture, and often brought him the message that he was expected for a meal at the Gertner hearth.

It was in mid-September, two months after Frau Gertner had been delivered of a healthy baby girl, that Meisterin summoned Lena to her quarters once more.

"You are doing well in your work with the Gertners," she began "Frau Gertner has expressed great satisfaction in your handling of both Bernhard and the new baby. She also very much appreciates your help in the household."

"Thank you," Lena murmured.

"However," Meisterin continued, taking hold of a letter which lay on her desk, "there is some matter which I must discuss with you, a matter of great import."

"Yes?"

"I have here a document, sent to me by the prior of the Strasbourg Dominicans, which indicates that not Agatha Lichtenberg, but one born Jurgen Ostermeier, also a Dominican, is your guardian. I believe, he was the cousin who called a number of months ago."

"Cousin, yes. But guardian he is not. Indeed, he is not," Lena vehemently cried out, "My father liked him not, so how could he be?"

"Well, this document states that he is," Meisterin said very matter-of-factly, "and I must act accordingly. The prior states, unequivocally, that it was your father's wish that you enter a convent."

"That is not true," Lena began, "It was not at all his wish that I...."

"Yet," Meisterin interrupted, softening her voice, "I will not act on the document immediately. I will give you a few days to inquire as to the validity of this document. But if you cannot disprove it, I have no choice but to turn you over to the care of Jurgen Ostermeier."

Sister Gertrude heard Lena cry most of that night, but she could not get the girl to confide in her and it was with a heavy heart that she watched Lena set off for the Gertner's the next day. Bernhard noted immediately that Lena was out of sorts. She rubbed the salve onto his neck with such vigor that he winced.

"You're hurting me, Lena."

She kissed his face and professed remorse.

"I'm sorry, Bernhard."

"What is the matter, Lena?"

"I...," she began, and repeated, "I...."

And then, much to Bernard's dismay, Lena began to cry, not even stopping when he wrapped his arms around her and said that after all, she had not hurt his neck very much, and she was the best friend he had ever had. Then, alarmed because her sobbing seemed to increase rather than decrease, he called his mother. It was only after a drink of water and much patting on the back that Lena calmed down.

"Can you tell me what is the matter, child?"

"I," Lena began, still hiccuping slightly after her bout of weeping, "I have to go into a convent."

"A convent?"

Frau Gertner and Bernhard spoke simultaneously.

"Yes," Lena repeated, "a convent. My cousin Jurgen is with the Dominicans and they have sent a paper to the beguinage saying that I am his ward and that my father left explicit instructions that I should enter a convent."

"But is this true?" Frau Gertner asked anxiously, "Did your father leave such instructions? The Dominicans are very powerful. Although many monastic clergy have deserted their monasteries in the last few years, there are still those that have a lot of power."

"No, it is not true! My father did not want me in a convent. He instructed me to listen to the new preachers, even," she went on in a less vehement voice, "as I have been doing."

"Then how comes it about that such a document..."

Frau Jurgen stopped, bewildered.

"It is likely a forged paper," Lena said, "but who am I, an orphan alone in the world, to disprove such a matter. Cousin Jurgen will, in all likelihood, be proved right and I ...."

She broke off and tears formed in her eyes again.

"I'm sure," Frau Gertner said softly, "that something will happen. Remember Lena that you recently professed to me your love for Jesus? Remember that you said you believed He died for you? Would such a Savior let you be sent to a convent where you would not hear His blessed words taught anymore?"

Frau Gertner's gentle discourse grew very much louder as she spoke and she emphatically added the words, "Not if I can help it."

Overcome by misery, the girl did not answer her. Frau Gertner tried again.

"Who is Jesus, Lena?"

"He is ...," Lena's words were barely audible, "is God, Who became man so that He might come and save me. He became a little child, just as I was."

Her voice grew just a bit stronger at this point and she went on.

"He learned from His earthly father, Joseph, and from His mother, Mary. Jesus was a carpenter like His earthly father and worked with His hands. But later, He died for our sins, so that He could hold us in His hands forever."

Lena held out her hand and Frau Gertner took it.

"Indeed, well spoken! Remember that, child. He holds you in His hand always. And now I shall send word to the beguinage that you are needed here this night. Then we can speak to Herr Gertner, who will be home this evening, and perhaps he can think of something that we might contrive to help you out of this quandary."

Balthazar Gertner was a large man and a kindly one. When he laughed, his belly shook, as did the table. But when he heard of the nature of Lena's problem, his face became grave.

"You haven't seen the document?" he queried Lena.

She shook her head.

"It was probably most unwise of me not to ask Meisterin to see it," she replied, "But I did not."

"We can go to a lawyer," he said, "but that will cost us money."

"I have some money," Lena stated in a rather straightforward manner, "and it is that money which cousin Jurgen wants. But it is at the beguinage. I have hidden it. My father left it to me and Agatha gave it to me when she brought me to Strasbourg."

"How much money?" Herr Gertner asked.

"Fifty gold coins," she said.

"Fifty gold coins?" he repeated a trifle disbelievingly, "Are you sure?"

When she nodded, he went on, "Such a sum is more than enough to pay a lawyer. But you will have to go back to the beguinage to retrieve it. Do you want me to go with you tomorrow?"

She nodded again, much relieved at his proposal.

"Very well, then. We will proceed to retain a lawyer, and," he smiled at her, "we will succeed with God's help."

The next morning, Herr Gertner and Lena, with Bernhard waving from the window, set off for the beguinage. It was a blustery, dark and rainy day. Lena recalled the first time she had walked towards the beguinage with Agatha. That had been some half year prior to this. At that time, the beguinage courtyard had seemed peaceful and quiet, whereas now it felt wet and cold. The flowers, dead and bedraggled in the early autumn, boded distress and Lena felt her heart hammer so hard that surely Herr Gertner must hear it. He, even as Agatha had done before, rang the bronze bell attached to the wall. When the portress, sister Adelgard, opened the door, he introduced himself as Lena's employer and asked if he might see Meisterin. It had been agreed upon, that while Herr Gertner saw Meisterin, Lena was to go to her room, extract the money from the wall niche, and wait for Herr Gertner in the courtyard.

Sister Adelgard showed Herr Gertner, who was all compliments and smiles, to Meisterin's quarters.

Consequently, the portress paid little attention to Lena who fairly flew to her own room. But when she opened the door, stepping over the threshold, she was horrified to find cousin Jurgen standing at the foot of sister Gertrude's bed. Lying open-mouthed, sister Gertrude's breathing was little more than a rattle, and her eyes were closed. Cousin Jurgen swiveled his head towards Lena as she entered.

"Well, Lena."

His voice was hoarse, gritty almost. Sister Gertrude moaned at the sound. Her closed eyes opened to half-slits. Lena took a step towards the bed.

"Is she ill? Is sister Gertrude ill?"

"She is dying. Meisterin sent a messenger early this morning asking me to come and administer the last rites. I was about to do just that."

Sister Gertrude's eyes suddenly opened wide. They stared at Lena with a piercing look, a look which made her uncomfortable.

"You must use the money, Lena," sister Gertrude's voice was very soft, but also very compelling, "You must use the money."

Cousin Jurgen dug a thin, claw-like hand into the burse which was hanging around his neck from a cord. Taking out the pyx, he placed it on the table right next to the bed. Then he genuflected to the pyx. Next he took a container out of his cassock, a container holding what the Catholic church called 'holy water', and began sprinkling it around himself.

"Sister Gertrude?" Lena whispered.

Sister Gertrude did not open her eyes, but she did repeat, very softly but raspingly clearly, "The money, give the priest the money, Lena. For then he will say prayers for me... please, Lena!"

Cousin Jurgen threw Lena a menacing look before he took his place on the right side of the bed, next to sister Gertrude.

"I have come to administer extreme unction," he began, "Do you want to confess, daughter?"

The words rolled out smoothly and rapidly, as if he were in a hurry to administer the sacrament and get it over with. Lena stood very still. The coverlet on the bed moved up and down, up and down. Sister Gertrude's breathing was very labored.

"Do you want to confess to me, daughter?" cousin Jurgen repeated.

It seemed that at this point, sister Gertrude had gone beyond speaking. There was only wheezing. Her nostrils flared and her color was pasty. Cousin Jurgen stared at the prostrate woman for several minutes. Then he spoke.

"It would be wrong of me to put the host on her lips. I do not know if she is able to swallow at this point."

He turned sideways suddenly, so that his back was not to the host, for it was considered wrong, Lena knew, to turn one's back to the host. Again glaring at Lena malevolently, he hissed words at her.

"Do you not know that it is wicked to withhold money from a dying woman who wishes the church to say prayers for her? Surely you know that anyone who commits such a wicked sin will have to pay a heavy penance."

Lena did not respond.

"Very well, then," cousin Jurgen went on, "I have warned you!"

Turning his back to her, he reached into his cassock taking out a vial holding a thick liquid. Lena knew the liquid, *oleum infirmorum*, was a specially mixed oil for those who needed supernatural assistance in dying. Cousin Jurgen poured the viscous fluid onto his right thumb as he held the small container sideways. He then leaned over and put his thumb onto sister Gertrude's forehead.

"Through this holy anointing may the Lord in His love and mercy help You with the grace of the Holy Spirit."

The oil dribbled down sister Gertrude's face and Lena had an inordinate desire to wipe it off. Surely it would tease and offend her skin. Cousin Jurgen poured some more oil onto his thumb and anointed sister Gertrude's palms.

"May the Lord Who frees you from your sins, save you and raise you up."

Now he was finished. Carefully putting the vial back into his cassock, he walked towards the table. After genuflecting to it, he put the pyx back into the burse around his neck. Then he once more faced Lena.

"I think," he began in a smooth voice, "that you and I ought to have a little talk."

"No," she responded, "sister Gertrude has been dealt with, and now you are free to leave so that I might spend some time with her. And if you do not leave," she went on, "I shall call out for the other sisters."

Walking towards the door, she opened it and curtsied slightly as he passed her, inwardly breathing a sigh of relief that he truly was leaving.

At this point Sister Gertrude moaned and Lena glanced back towards the bed. She was horrified to see that her old roommate had her eyes wide open. Not only that, she winked at Lena, a cross-eyed wink, as she called out with a feeble, grainy voice.

"Brother Jurgen, please come back."

Not at all loath to do so, cousin Jurgen did an about-face from the open doorway. Smiling ingratiatingly, he sidled back up to the bed.

"Yes, sister Gertrude?"

"The girl will show you," the ancient voice rasped, "show you where the niche is where she has hidden her money and my money. If she does not...," and here sister Gertrude was overcome by a paroxysm of phlegmy coughing.

Cousin Jurgen's smile grew in proportion to the greed in his eyes. Lena stood perplexed as the priest eyed her balefully. Behind his back-sister Gertrude stopped coughing long enough to grin mawkisly at the girl. Shrugging and sighing simultaneously, Lena walked over to the wall. With her right hand she pushed the brick behind which she knew her gold to be hidden. The opening cavity revealed two bags - hers and sister Gertrude's. The priest's eager hands slipped past hers.

"I'll take these."

Carrying the bags to the table he emptied them onto the wood. Coins clattered out - bronze coins from sister Gertrude's bag and gold ones from Lena's. Open-mouthed the girl watched - watched and counted. Several times she counted and each time the sum from her own bag came to five gold coins, not fifty. Five gold coins lay flat and mute, glittering against the brown wood of the table. Cousin Jurgen fingered the gold. Lena could see him pondering.

"Well?" sister Gertrude's hoarse whisper interrupted his thoughts, "are there enough coins for my prayers, priest?"

"Yes, indeed," cousin Jurgen answered slowly, lifting his gaze from the coins to the bed.

"And the girl must stay here to care for me," the voice wheezed on, "as I shall not be long for...."

Sister Gertrude's quest trailed off, and her eyes were closed once more.

"For now," cousin Jurgen replied, "that is well. Yes, that is well."

Making a sweeping motion with his right hand, he cleared the table of the money, emptying them into the pocket of his cassock.

"And now I must go," he went on, "but I shall be back in a few hours to see how you fare. Or," he added, "I shall send another brother. It is no matter. We all serve the church."

Sister Gertrude commenced to moaning painfully, and Lena took a step towards the bed. The priest slipped past her again, so near that she could smell his sour breath.

"Farewell for now, cousin," he whispered, but she did not respond.

The door closed behind him and Lena contemplated what had just occurred. She could not fathom it. Then, just as she was trying to decide whether or not to go into the hall and look for Herr Gertner, sister Gertrude sat up, flung away the covers from her scrawny form, swung her thin legs over the edge of the bed and sat up. And all around her on the mattress lay gold pieces. There were everywhere these coins, mixed into the crumples and creases of the sheet and of her nightgown.

"Whatever...?," Lena began and stopped and then added, "How...?"

"It was simple," sister Gertrude explained between guffaws and coughs, "I knew I had to stop him from pestering you. He was always here asking questions, always on the lookout how he might get his fat hands on your inheritance, so I thought if he gets a little money... just a little, it might put him off the scent."

Lena was at her side in an instant after this explanation, putting her arms around the old lady. She kissed her, not at all minding the wart. To her surprise, the woman began to weep.

"You," she sobbed, "have been kinder to me than many, girl. Why should I not help you against that wheedling fat...."

A knock on the door stopped her short. Both women were startled into quiet. Sister Gertrude quickly tucked her legs back under the covers, hiding the gold. Lena slowly went to answer the knock. To her relief, the caller was Herr Gertner.

"May I come in?"

"Of course," Lena said, glancing hesitantly over her shoulder at sister Gertrude.

But sister Gertrude lay with her eyes close, seemingly dead to the world.

"Is she...?"

Herr Gertner let the question dangle.

"No, no," Lena answered quickly, "She is only sleeping."

"Well," Herr Gertner continued softly, "Meisterin says you might come and spend the night with us. I told her we wanted a lawyer to look at the document and she willingly allowed me to take it with me. Only, I had to promise to return it to her tomorrow."

Lena nodded.

"But from what I have seen of it, child," Herr Gertner spoke very gravely now, "it certainly appears genuine. I fear we shall need some good advice to get you out of the clutches of that money-hungry cousin of yours. Were you able to get the money of which you spoke?"

At this point sister Gertrude opened her eyes and sat up. Herr Gertner was slightly taken aback. She smiled sweetly at him, cross-eyed, wart trembling, even as she reached under the covers exposing the gold coins. For all her nervousness and anxiety, Lena began to laugh. After a moment, sister Gertrude's cackle joined her, and then Herr Gertner's belly-booming bass mixed in with the women's merriment.

Later that evening, as Herr and Frau Gertner sat at table together with Lena and Herr Schatzer, the lawyer, they marvelled at the events of the day.

"I have learned," Lena spoke softly, "that God is truly One Who works in miraculous ways."

Frau Gertner nodded and warmly smiled at her.

"Yes, He is."

"I'm afraid though," Herr Schatzer spoke, papers in front of him, "that this document which you have brought back appears quite authentic. Brother Jurgen is clearly shown to be your sole surviving relative."

His voice and his being oozed authority and everyone fell morosely silent. Lena stared at the tablecloth. A few moments ago, she had been full of faith, hoping against hope that all would be well. The rich fabric of the tablecloth danced in front of her eyes. Herr Schatzer cleared his voice.

"There is a loophole," he added.

From the tablecloth, Lena peered down at the hands which lay folded in her lap. They had begun to tremble.

"That loophole is...", Herr Schatzer continued slowly in a low baritone, and then stopped because at that moment there was a loud knock at the front door.

Lena's hands tightened on one another. Would that be cousin Jurgen come to claim his guardianship? No, it could not be. Meisterin had said they could have a few days to sort things out. Herr Gertner rose to answer. Frau Gertner reached over and patted Lena's shoulder.

"Don't worry, child," she encouraged, "you are presently quite safe here."

Lena smiled wanly. After all the events which had occurred today should she not be thankful? It took some ten minutes before Herr Gertner came back into the room. He was followed by Paul Josselin.

"I'm really sorry to intrude. I stopped by the house to ask Herr Gertner something about a carpentry project, and then he..., " Paul began, "that is to say, he told me that...."

Stopping, his voice became softer as he caught Lena's eye and he went on slower and in a deeper tone.

"... that you were in trouble, Lena, and I wanted to offer my help."

"Please sit down, Paul," Frau Gertner said, "we are glad you are here."

He took the chair opposite Lena, all the while holding her gaze with a gentle smile.

"Herr Schatzer was about to tell us of the possibility of a loophole," Herr Gertner posited, "which might aid Lena. Were you not, Herr Schatzer?"

"Yes, I was," the lawyer responded.

"Well," Frau Gertner said in a rather breathless voice, when Herr Schatzer did not immediately continue, "please let us know what, in your estimation, the chances are of Lena's freedom."

The lawyer smiled at her.

"It is difficult to phrase," he started, "but it comes down to this. If Lena were married, certainly a husband's right of guardianship would override that of a second cousin."

"Married?" Frau Gertner repeated.

"Married?" Lena whispered.

In agitation, her trembling hands moved from her lap onto the table. They lay alone. There was no way out. She had feared this. In spite of the money, inspite of the help of these dear people, she would fall into the hands of... But at that moment, her hands were enfolded by someone else, by someone sitting across the table from her - by a carpenter.

"Would you be content to become my wife, Lena?"

Paul Josselin spoke the words out loud, oblivious of everyone but Lena.

And she, all tears and doubts dissolving, stared at her covered hands.

The Boy that Drove the Plow

"If God spare my life, ere many years pass, I will cause the boy that driveth the plow to know more of the Scripture than thou dost" *(Tyndale).*

The Severn burbled alongside its banks. Longer than the Thames and famous for its tidal bore, the river's source lay in the moorlands of mid-Wales and its murky depths flowed past the city of Gloucester in three separate channels. There was the western channel; the easternmost channel, also known as the Little Severn; and the formidable middle channel, the one carrying the greatest volume of water, known as the Great Severn. The middle channel was spanned by Westgate Bridge, the longest bridge in England and one much prized by all Gloucester citizens for it brought much business to the area. It was the route over which much merchandise passed - merchandise such as wood, salt, cloth, corn, wine and cattle. It was also one of the the pathways over which new thoughts and ideas crept into the city.

It was 1537. Thomas Drourie, a cattleman, reflected on these matters one early October morning as he guided his herd of cows along the crossover. Dark currents swirled about below him. Drourie was a tall man, and for that reason was considered prosperous. The height of most men in Gloucester averaged five and a half feet. Thomas' over six foot stature was imposing. Yet when he smiled, the measure of his towering frame radiated friendliness. Dark of hair and swarthy of face, he was a lean, strong fellow, one who embodied hard work and resilience.

The hoofbeats of the cows echoed hollowly on the thick wooden slats. Trekking between his cattle, Thomas bellowed out a noisy, tuneless ditty. He'd noted his animals enjoyed music for when he hummed or sang during milking, the full udders spouted a greater amount of milk into his pails. The bridge groaned and creaked with the collective weight of the party. Storms and flooding often wreaked damage on its timber anatomy. Almost a citizen itself, the Westgate was considered so dear to Gloucester, that often folks would leave a bequest for its upkeep and repair.

"Thomas!"

Startled, he stopped his singing. Turning sideways, he peered down into the face of a Franciscan priest who had managed to edge in next to him between the cattle. The man flanked Thomas, although his plump form in its loose-flapping, wide-sleeved cassock barely reached the height of the farmer's shoulders. The man was afflicted, Thomas thought to himself as he always did when he saw the cleric, with belly-cheer, with gluttony.

"I haven't seen you at Mass for a while, Thomas."

The words were calmly but loudly spoken, as need be, for the commotion of the cattle made soft talk impossible. Thomas gave no answer, but calmly continued walking, steering his animals towards the Northgate Street. He knew

Father Serly, for this was the name of the priest, would turn towards Westgate Street, where St. Nicholas' Church stood at its far end and where he and a number of other friars resided.

"Thomas!"

Father Serly's voice was more intense now and no longer neutral.

"It's been busy."

It was the only answer Thomas voiced before turning onto Northgate.

There were four main roads leading in and out of Gloucester, all meeting at a main intersection where the town's high cross stood. All were named from the gates by which they entered town. Thus there were the Eastgate, Northgate, Southgate and Westgate streets. Northgate led to London; Southgate to Bristol; Eastgate to Oxford; and Westgate to Wales. People walked, rode in carts, and journeyed by horse on these unpaved roads. Some four thousand citizens made their home in Gloucester.

Passing the Tolsey, the town hall, Thomas longingly eyed the nearby New Inn. Its strong, massive external galleries and courtyards attracted pilgrims and visitors alike. How he yearned to go into the public house and drink some of its frothing ale for he was thirsty after his long morning walk. But with these newly bought cows as his companions, he was forced to amble past the gabled and timbered structure, well aware that the priest probably still stood at the crossroad, eyeing his retreating form suspiciously.

The truth was that Thomas held no high opinion of the local priests, or of any priests for that matter, and only occasionally attended Mass. A devoted cattle-man, he spent much time on his farm, waxing poetic to anyone who would listen, about the state of his cows, calves, and steers. Praising their rich, dark brown color, he often remarked with a twinkle in his eyes, that the color resembled the tint of Dory's hair. And wasn't she a beauty? Dory was his wife. The bulls in his herd, on the other hand, hued a blue-black shade, and while showing them off he would point to his own hair and grin. All of the Drourie cattle sported white bellies and were finch-backed. That is to say, they all had a white finching stripe along their spine, a stripe which continued on over the tail. Well-developed horns with black tips crowned their heads. Thomas Drourie was inordinately proud of his livestock. Noted for providing strong and docile draught oxen, the beasts also proved to be tender beef when roasted on the spit. As well, they were valued for the richness of their milk. The fat in that milk made a full, hard cheese - cheese with a buttery, mellow, nutty taste. Thomas sold it at the Gloucester market on Westgate Street. Aged for four months, double Gloucester cheese was popular throughout the region.

Lizzie Drourie was born later that same day. Arriving home, Thomas learned that Janey, the midwife, had been closeted in the bedroom with Dory all night. A tinge of fear shivered through his stomach. By his calculations, it was a trifle early for the child to be born.

"We had to send for her about an hour after you left yesterday to pick up the cows at Noent, master. But it's over now," Nelly, the kitchen maid, assured him, "Janey just came down before you came home to say all's well and that you were free to come up."

Indeed, it was all well, and he relaxed moments later at the bedside of his Dory, his long legs sprawled out under the great bed. She looked weary, mounds of her dark brown hair spread across the pillow. But though her face was exhausted, it was also contented and he was lost in admiration of her.

"It's a girl, Thomas," she whispered, "a bonny girl, and I'd like to name her Elizabeth."

He was of a mind to let her have whatever she wanted and nodded in agreement.

"Lizzie, then," he answered softly.

Janey tutted as she bustled about, carrying the swaddled newborn. A moment later, Thomas curiously peered into the tightly bound bundle she laid into his arms and he suddenly recalled with some alarm that it had been this very day a year ago that William Tyndale had been burned at the stake. He said as much even as he was overcome by the dark eyes of his firstborn daughter. But the memory of Tyndale somehow clouded the joy.

"It's a bad omen for the child," he added after contemplating Lizzie.

"Oh, tush," responded Janey, who had little ken of such as Tyndale, "the child is beautiful, your wife is doing well, and you're just a bit daft not to note it."

Dory smiled, and Thomas grudgingly had to admit that all seemed exceptionally propitious with both mother and child. So after sitting a while, stroking his wife's hand and intermittently peering into the cradle where Lizzie had been laid, he left the birthing room for the stable where there was ample room to stretch his legs. And as the door shut behind him, Janey commented disdainfully that recalling the death of someone they had not even known, was ridiculous.

"But," Dory protested weakly, her mind mostly on the fact that she had just born her first child, "Master Tyndale was, after all, a Gloucester man, Janey. He was from our area. It seems clear to me that all he wanted to do was give the English people the Bible to read. And although I have not read it for myself, I cannot help but think that such a gift had no evil intent. They say that Queen Anne," she added a moment later, "the poor lass who was executed last year, had a small Bible, a richly ornamented one, and that she wrote the words 'Anna Regina Angliae' around its edges."

It was a long sentence, a bit of a ramble, and she yawned towards the end.

"We've no need to read the Bible, lass," the midwife cheerfully responded, "Why we've got the pope, haven't we, to tell us what we need to know?"

"Yes, but," Dory rejoined, her thoughts becoming fuzzier, "now that King Henry has made himself the head of the church, we haven't got the pope any more, have we? Besides that, I once saw master Tyndale here in Gloucester. He was giving alms to a beggar, and seemed to me to be a most kind and gentle man."

After these words, totally drained of her physical energy, she fell asleep. For a brief minute before she continued her cleaning up, Janey stood at the foot of the bed, smiling tender-heartedly at the sight of the spent, young woman. Then she continued her tasks, muttering softly to herself that King Henry was not really interested in being the head of the church and surely everyone in England knew it. Was it not obvious that the man was only interested in power? And that which mostly occupied his waking days was passing that power on to a male heir. His third wife, Queen Jane, was about to give birth shortly and hadn't English people like herself been instructed to pray for the child to be a son? Wouldn't it be something to be the midwife in Hampton Court palace this month? Oh, well, Janey philosophized, even as she tucked a woolen coverlet around the newborn Lizzie, it really wasn't any of her concern. Then she smiled into Lizzie's wide-open, dark eyes.

"I stand to benefit from your birth, little one," she whispered to the baby, "and isn't that the truth of it! I'll be needed for a goodly while as your mother regains her strength, and the extra income is most welcome to me. I've six moppets at home and their appetite is as large as your father is tall."

Lizzie blinked and Janey smiled again.

In those days the meadowlands embracing Gloucester were dotted with farms. One of these was the Drourie farm. Comprising two hundred acres, more than half of it was arable, quite suitable for growing crops. Most of the remaining land was meadow with some woodland included. Thomas grew enough produce to feed his cattle. He also bred fine animals, made cheese and sold what he did not need at market. It was good way to live, he reflected as he stroked the finching stripe of one of the cows. Feeling rather emotional because of Lizzie's birth, he preached softly to the animal.

"There is a time to be born," he murmured, "and a time to die. This is Lizzie's time to live."

The cow lowed softly in response and Thomas ground his foot into the hay reflecting that it was perhaps not wise to think beyond what one could know. This daughter, this brand new Lizzie, might live a long, long life, and he fervently hoped that she would, but he should not presume. She might also be followed by more children. Perhaps he would have a son in the years to come, a strong son who would take over the farm when he himself became too old. Lizzie as well, when she grew older, could help around the house and Dory could teach her to become proficient in the cheese making. He smiled to himself and Albert, the young stable hand, watched his master aimlessly fork some hay into the loft. Albert was only twelve, but a strong, strapping lad.

The small but handsome, granite farm house was an inheritance which had been conferred on Thomas by his grandfather. Endowed with demesne, land attached and retained for the owner's use, the two-storied home had a large kitchen, a bower room, and several side rooms. The projecting porch even boasted a parvise – an enclosed area surrounded by colonnades. The porch also led into a fine hall where the family ate. There were mullioned windows, oak-panelled walls and a sizeable fireplace. The premises suited Thomas and Dory very well, and they employed five servants all of whom loved and respected them.

The district surrounding Gloucester was not only dotted with farms, it was also dotted with Articles, six articles, to be exact. Written by the king, these specific rules reminded the English who was in charge - not the Pope who lived in Italy, but Henry VIII who lived in England. Still a Roman Catholic at heart, however, Henry's first article insisted that his subjects continue to adhere to transubstantiation - the conversion of the bread at Mass into the actual body and blood of Christ. The penalty for not believing this was death by burning at the stake.

Thomas Drourie sometimes pondered transubstantiation as he took care of his cattle. The word was as long as a cow's tail. Why the king should care that he, Thomas Drourie, should believe this was a mystery to him. One way or the other, would he not be the same English farmer? Stroking the side of a cow, he grimaced at the thought of church attendance. He liked not the priests that served the Eucharist and he avoided going to Mass. Besides that, there were new ideas coming to the fore in Gloucester, Protestant ideas. Thomas and his fellow citizens were well aware of them. Many deep, and often heated, discussions took place in the New, the Boatman, the Ram, the Bull, the Swan, and other inns in Gloucester. There were open disputes about Roman Catholic doctrine along the English countryside and in the city. Lately a local weaver attending St. Mary de Crypt church on Southgate Street, had denied the doctrine of purgatory because he believed that the Bible did not teach it. Irritably Thomas slapped the cow's buttocks and the animal turned its head, fixing its great eyes on her master. Thomas paid no heed. His thoughts wandered on. Although he had no stomach for disagreements, he liked neither the church's nor the king's ways. Was it not so that the king also had a child named Lizzie, a little maid all of four years old? And did this child not wander around all alone in the royal palace because her mother had been first divorced and then beheaded? Ah, his own small Lizzie, although not a princess, was much more blessed. Did she not have a father to love her and a Dory to care for her?

Lizzie Drourie was an only child for the first five years of her life. Strangely enough, the year after her birth, King Henry issued a royal license that the Bible might openly be sold to and read by all English people without any danger of recrimination. Another royal order was issued as well, appointing a copy of the Bible to be placed in every parish church. It was to be raised upon a desk so that everyone might come and read it. Overnight Gloucester Abbey became Gloucester Cathedral. Clergy replaced the monks not just in Gloucester, but in all the monasteries and convents throughout England, Wales and Ireland. Disbanded, their incomes were appropriated for the crown. Any resistance was viewed as treasonable. Under heavy threats almost all of the religious houses joined the new English church swearing to uphold the King's divorce and remarriage.

Gloucester Cathedral acquired a Bible also. John Wakeman, the first Bishop of Gloucester, made sure it was placed in an accessible spot and soon citizens cautiously dropped by for a look. Thomas and Dory came as well. Those who were able bought the book from printers, book sellers, or traveling tinkers. If they could not read, and many could not, they persuaded others to read Scripture to them. How different, Thomas and Dory pondered, had been the years before Lizzie's birth. At that time anyone wishing to read the Bible had to do so secretly.

It was not until just before their second child was born, that Thomas and Dory also purchased a Bible from Philip, a traveling tinker. They'd known Philip for a long time, for he was wont to stop by their farm once or twice every year. A versatile man, his cart was filled with all manner of things. Carrying a pocketful of news about current events, he was also well-versed in languages, music and Scripture. Thomas, who could read, was much taken with the newly-bought Bible. Sitting Lizzie upon his knees, in the evenings he read out loud to the child and to Dory. He did not understand all he read, but he felt privileged to be reading. Dory listened attentively from her easy chair by the fire and rubbed her swollen stomach. Another Drourie child grew large within her belly. She wondered if the baby could hear any of the beautiful words which Thomas read. Leaning back, she smiled contentedly. They had never before heard the Bible in their own language.

On the day Dory went into labor, Thomas sent Albert, who was now almost seventeen, to fetch Janey the midwife and gave instructions to the dairy maid to take Lizzie to the bower room and keep her occupied, away from her mother. Janey, arriving shortly afterwards, first made sure all the doors were unlocked. She explained that it was an old custom and aided childbirth. Thomas was in two minds about this, but Janey insisted. And indeed, it proved to be an easy birth. The boy child, although tiny, appeared healthy. Janey bathed the little, red body before an ash wood lit fire. Afterwards she had him suckle on a cloth dipped in cinder tea, water into which a coal had been dropped. When she saw Thomas staring, she explained good-naturedly that all knew this drove Satan away.

"I don't recall you doing that when Lizzie was born," Thomas commented as he watched her, rather uneasy about the matter as it smacked of superstition.

"But you weren't there all the time, now were you, Master Thomas," she replied calmly, "and haven't things been well with that lass?"

Speaking to himself in an undertone, Thomas strode over and lifted the newborn out of Janey's arms, pulling the cloth out of the baby's blackening mouth.

"Enough now," he said, "there are other things your hands can find to do. And one of them is to tell Albert to distribute bread, cheese and ale to the poor of Gloucester. Go on with you and I'll stay with Dory and the babe."

His son whimpered in his arms. The face was red and wrinkled, minding Thomas of his old deceased grandfather. Sitting down by the bed, he studied his wife. Two children she had now born him. He was a rich man indeed. Dory was almost asleep but she opened her eyes and smiled at him.

"We'll name him Thomas for you. But it must be little Thomas, for you are so much bigger."

And that is how the boy became known throughout Gloucester.

During his first year, Little Thomas drank sporadically and was prone to mewling. Excessive crying caused discoloration around his eyes. Janey concocted a solution of nightshade sap, soaked a clean rag in it and laid it on the baby's eyes.

"Perhaps he has cramps," Dory ventured to guess, "I've heard that laying babies down flat and pulling their legs straight can help them belch?"

But Janey only smiled at her.

Lizzie proved to be a most helpful and patient sister, though she herself was still a child. Rocking her brother for hours on end, she often changed his clout, sang to him and kissed him.

"She is a better mother than I am," Dory confided to Thomas, "and has the patience of a saint. I heard her say the other day 'Little Thomas, I won't ever leave you, even if you cry for a year'.

Thomas smiled.

"He will grow out of this crying and this colic, Dory," he promised, "Just wait and see."

It was true. By the time Little Thomas turned toddler, he was thriving; and when the child turned six, although still small of stature, he was so full of mischief that the scullery maid was in fear of him. Intensely curious, he was also a naïve boy. Once, after cook had wrung the necks of several pigeons in preparation for squab pie, leaving them in the kitchen on the table, she came back to find the boy holding onto one of the dead birds. There was blood all over his hands, shirt and breeches.

"And what do you think you're doing?" she asked.

"I thought perhaps," he answered with a child's logic, "that if you wrung the neck the other way, the pigeon might come back to life."

Then he proceeded to do just that. Shocked, the cook took the bird out of his hands.

"Growing chuff-headed, are you? Away with you," she retorted, "or I'll put you into the pie as well."

Little Thomas loved Philip the tinker and often followed him about the farm when he came to call. Because Philip was kind and exemplary of character, Thomas and Dory did not mind in the least. They hoped the tinker would nousle little Thomas in piety. The truth was that Philip was a highly educated man. Able to read and write, as well as play the viol, Thomas and Dory eventually asked him to become their son's tutor.

Just prior to Little Thomas' birth, Henry VIII had founded a boy's school in Gloucester. Previously there had been a school in the Abbey of St. Peter, but because all monasteries had been closed, that school no longer functioned. The headmaster of the new school was a solemn man and one who exacted strict obedience. Because of his impishness, continual misdemeanors and disregard for authority, Little Thomas was not a favored student. The boy was, in fact, not fitting in very well at the school at all, and frequently in trouble with the headmaster. This pained Thomas and Dory greatly for little Thomas was a gifted child. His almost photographic memory enabled him not only to read well, but also to quote Latin and Scripture texts at will. The boy's greatest offence had been climbing the bell tower with some friends, and swinging the clapper loudly during a service, thus bringing shame on himself and his family. He had capped that escapade by putting a duck egg under the cover of the headmaster's bed and by hanging the man's pantofles from the branch of a tree a week later. The headmaster did not want to see him back for at least a year, or until, as he had gravely said to Dory and Thomas, such a time as the boy had learned to unquestioningly obey rules and regulations.

Thomas, who had let his son feel the backside of his hand on more than one occasion, was at his wits end. Several times neighbors had suggested that little Thomas was heading towards pravity and that his parents must see to it that he was disciplined or he would turn into a runagate. It was at precisely this time that Dory and Thomas asked Philip if he would stay and tutor the child. After some careful consideration Philip agreed to do this for a while, thus becoming, for a time anyway, a permanent resident of the Drourie farm.

Change was blowing through England during the Drourie children's early formative years. In 1547 King Henry VIII died and was carried to his grave in pomp and splendor. Edward VI, Henry's son, was crowned in his place. Although only nine years old, Edward had been nursed by Protestant teachers and his youthful heart was warmly turned towards the Reformation. A child richly used by God, one of the first things young Edward did was to overturn his father's Six Articles.

A few years Edward's ascent to the throne, little Thomas turned both eleven and more obdurate. It was the same year that a Dr. Williams preached in one of the churches in Gloucester. The boy, who attended church regularly with his father, mother, Lizzie and Philip, heard him speak. Dr. Williams was the city's chancellor. A recent convert to Protestantism, he had publicly chosen the Protestant faith over the Catholic faith.

It is strange how God uses men's words to change hearts, even very young hearts. And so it was on the day on which

Dr. Williams preached, that little Thomas, for so he was still known, was transformed.

"The sacrament," so Dr. Williams solemnly echoed forth from the fine pulpit as he spoke about the sacrament of Mass, "is to be received spiritually by faith. It is not to be received carnally as the papists have heretofore taught."

Now these were difficult words, and yet Little Thomas repeated them verbatim to Philip, his new teacher, as they were out walking together.

"What think you, Master Philip," he asked, "that these words mean?"

The tinker did not respond immediately. But after some thirty or so steps, he finally answered.

"First of all, I think that we must never in our thoughts or words, pity the Lord Jesus for dying on the cross."

The child looked up at him questioningly. He did not understand.

"To pity someone," the tinker went on, "is to place yourself on a higher level. Our Savior Jesus Christ, is Lord overall and never on a lower level than we are. What think you? That we can make Him bread and kill Him again and again? He died once, child, and that willingly, of His own accord."

Overhead a lark, nondescript and brown, sang an extravagant melody.

"I think," Philip went on, "that it might help you to call to mind the time that Jesus was eating bread with His disciples in the Upper Room. Do you recall it?"

Little Thomas nodded.

"Picture in your mind then, their gathering around a wooden table, a table such as we eat from together in the great hall. Hear in your heart what Jesus said to them, and says to us now, as He broke the bread: "This is My body, which is for you; do this in remembrance of Me."

As they were speaking, the pair were traipsing through one of the fields adjoining the farm. Philip carried his viol case for the idea was that there was to be a music lesson out in the quiet of a pastureland. There were cattle grazing some distance away.

"Jesus did not mean that He was actually present in the bread, little Thomas. What Jesus meant was that whenever people would eat the bread in the future, they were to recollect, to remember, that He offered up His body. This He did on the cross shortly after that supper, child. And we are to remember this and to believe it."

Again, a melodious jumble of clear notes and trills rang through the sky overhead. The boy tilted his head up to gaze after the lark. The bird sang as it flew. Little Thomas stared up at the creature. He appeared to be not listening.

"To remember and believe that Christ died for you," the tinker went on, making his words simpler, even as he stood next to the child, "is to know that you have eternal life. And then you can joyfully sing even as yonder lark."

As the boy still remained quiet, he went on slowly, probing the heart.

"You are getting too old to be known as Little Thomas. I think I will call you Tom from now on. Do you believe what I have just told you, Tom?"

The child nodded and followed up the nodding with a question.

"Can we have a music lesson now, Master Philip?"

Now it was so, that Philip was proficient in viol playing and at Thomas' and Dory's request, he was beginning to pass this skill on to their son. A distant relative of the violin, the viol was a bowed instrument with frets. Flat-backed, it was played while set on the ground between a player's legs. Its tone was quiet but had a distinct, low quality. A gentleman's instrument, it was played in salons, whereas violins were more often played on streets to accompany dances or to lead in wedding processions. The Drouries hoped the learning of the viol might calm their child and stand him to good advantage.

Philip concurred with Tom's wish.

"Fine, child. Let us sit ourselves down on this log."

They had come to a small copse. A field lay in front of them and a forest behind them.

Philip took the viol out of its bag, and both the man and the child seated themselves on an old, fallen horse chestnut tree trunk lying in front of the thicket. It was quiet outside safe for the lowing of some distant cattle.

"Hold the bow," Philip instructed his pupil, propping up the instrument between the child's legs, "betwixt the end of your thumb and the two foremost fingers of your right hand."

Tom eagerly reached for the convex stick. He loved the music Philip often made as they sat evenings by the fireplace in the front room. The viol's body was light and the six strings seemed to him to be magical.

"Now fasten the thumb and first finger of your left hand on the stalk."

Philip knelt down in front of the boy. His hands instructed the much smaller hands - hands which began to work fearfully hard at contorting fingers to meet the requirements. It was difficult and awkward, because this was the first lesson. Through his concentration Tom thought he heard a snorting sound. Looking up over Philip's shoulder, his hands froze. One of his father's bulls, massive and terrifying, the black tips of its white horns aimed directly at them, was galloping through the meadow in their direction.

"Master Philip!" he gasped, "Look yonder."

Philip turned his head and immediately stood up. Taking the viol away from Tom, he commanded the lad to stand behind him and then to quickly walk backwards towards the nearby woodland. He himself sat down on the tree trunk, calmly placing the viol downwards between his legs. Glancing over his shoulder he saw that although Thomas was moving, he was moving slowly and woodenly.

"Obey me immediately," he ordered again, "Walk faster, Tom, walk faster, child. And find a tree behind which you can stand."

"What ... What about you?" the boy stuttered, tripping over both his words and his feet.

"I believe the bull is bellowing in a B flat and I shall try to outdo him," Philip answered and proceeded to draw his bow across the strings.

The low, quiet hum of the viol resonated across the field. It met the bull's wheezing midair. Though Tom was only some thirty feet away by this time, he stopped walking backwards at the same moment that he saw the bull stop charging. To his great amazement the boy beheld the animal shake its bulky head a few times and then peaceably turn around and amble away.

"Well now, you have learned two rather unique and wonderful things, Thomas," Philip said, when the boy was back at his side.

He kept playing as he spoke, sliding the bow over the strings, harmonious notes spilling onto the grass around and beyond like heavy raindrops.

"What?" the boy asked, his heart still thumping as he watched the backside of the massive bovine saunter away.

"Firstly that bulls do not like the key of B flat," smiled his teacher.

Tom grinned, although tremulously.

"And what is the second," he demanded a moment later.

"That Almighty God keeps an eye on those who call out to Him in trouble."

"Oh," replied Tom, "and did you call out?"

"Yes," accorded his teacher.

The boy stared off into the field. The bull was still in retreat and seemed to not even remember their existence. He sighed heavily and then grinned again, high spirits returning.

"I am sorry for one thing," he joked, "and that is that Lizzie was not here to see it, for she will never believe me when I tell her what happened.

That very evening Tom fell ill of a high fever. It charged at him even as the bull had run at them with lowered horns through the field. He thrashed about so much that he woke Lizzie who slept in the room next to his, and she, in turn woke her parents. In spite of the fact that prayers were raised and many herbal remedies applied, Tom was long in recuperating. His eyes seemed affected and discharged pus. Oozing continually, the boy could not open them. Though the fever abated after a few days, the infection lingered. Dory, Lizzie, and Philip took turns in sitting with the lad during the day. His father, although often looking in on his son during the day, sat with the boy at night. It became apparent to all of them, after a week or two, that the boy would not regain his sight.

"I have just received a small booklet, Tom."

The boy was sitting up in bed. Philip, who came and went at will, regarded the boy with affection.

"What is it?"

"It is a catechism written by a man named Alberus, Erasmus Alberus. He wrote it in German and he wrote it for his children. I know that you are rapidly approaching manhood, Tom, but I thought you might like to learn its questions and answers if I repeat them to you."

Tom nodded, his hands plucking at the blanket.

"Alberus wrote the booklet so that the important parts of Scripture might be learned by rote."

"Please let me learn also."

Startled, Philip turned and faced Thomas Drourie who stood in the doorway.

"I was not raised with Bible knowledge and often when I read, I do not understand what I am reading. Perhaps I can learn with you and we can speak of these matters."

It was a humble confession and Philip was moved. Tall and awkward, Thomas lumbered into the bedroom and sat on the edge of his son's bed. Philip smiled at him.

"Well, it would be fine for us to read and memorize together. I myself have added some questions and answers also."

So they proceeded with simple but very direct dialogues.

Do you love Jesus?

Yes.

Who is the Lord Jesus?

God and Mary's son.

How is His dear mother called?

Mary.

Why do you love Jesus? What has He done to make you love Him?

He has shed His blood for me.

Has he shed His blood only once or more than once as the Mass teaches?

Jesus has shed his blood only once on the cross at Calvary.

Could you be saved if He had not shed His blood for you?

Oh, no.

What would then have happened?

We would all be damned.

Is God's only begotten son, the son of the living God, your brother?

Yes.

So you are for sure a great and powerful king in heaven because Christ in heaven is your brother?

That I am, praise God.

How blessed you are! For the Lord has done a great thing for you.

Yes, He has. For He saves a poor, damned child from the Devil's kingdom and gave me eternal life.

The Drouries all benefited from these and other questions and answers which Philip taught them and many conversations took place around the bedside of the sick boy.

"Lizzie! Lizzie, I still can't see."

"I know. Hush, and lay down. If you move about too much, you will just get sicker again, Tom."

"Why are you calling me Tom, Lizzie?"

"Well, Master Philip says you are not little Thomas any longer. You have grown so. And I have heard Master Philip call you Tom, and mother and father call you that too now. So I think I will call you Tom."

"Will I never see again, Lizzie?"

The question was uttered in so plaintive a tone that Lizzie sighed.

"I hope you shall but I do not know."

"You are just being kind, are you not, Lizzie?"

Lizzie, sitting at her brother's bedside, reached over and kissed him.

"I shall always be there to be your eyes, Tom. I shall tell you everything I see."

"It won't be the same."

She knew that he was right but was not sure how to respond.

"I heard a new pastor preach in the cathedral, Tom. His name is John Hooper."

"He is not new, Lizzie," the boy replied, half-sitting up against the pillow, "he has been here for more than a year already."

"Oh," his sister said, disappointed that she could not tell him something he did not know, "and how would you have ken of that?"

"Master Philip has told me. He said John Hooper was called to preach before King Edward himself and that the king, who is only four years older than I am Lizzie, very much liked him and then made him Bishop of our city of Gloucester."

"Oh," Lizzie repeated.

"John Hooper," Tom went on, his hands fidgeting with the blanket, "is an honorable man and one who does not like to wear the rich garments that priests and other clergy wear. He says a man should dress humbly, even as your heart should be humble. So you will not see him clad in a chimere and rochet, such as other bishops wear, Lizzie."

She smiled at her brother and reached over again, patting his hand.

"You are all about clothing now, are you, Tom?"

He grinned for a minute and then teased her.

"And you are not? I have seen, when I could still see, how you constantly preen, Lizzie. And I know you do it for Albert. Only I do not know if father will allow you to marry him. He is after all, the hired hand."

Lizzie blushed and was glad for a moment that Tom could not see.

"But Tom is strong and a good lad," Tom continued, "And ... and I will not be able to help father plough now that I am, ... now that I am, ... well, now that I might be blind."

"Hush, Tom."

It was all Lizzie could say, for tears welled up in her eyes.

"Master Philip says that John Hooper, for all that he is the high and reverenced bishop of Gloucester, is a very good man."

It was quiet for a spell. Lizzie's thoughts turned to Albert, who was such a dependable young man, a hard-working man, a man on whom her father could count. Indeed, she did love him and admired him more than all the young men she knew. But father might object to their marriage, that Tom had indeed said rightly.

"Master Hooper," Tom's voice interrupted her contemplations, "has a wife and children, just like our father. His children, Master Philip says, are well mannered. It shames me, Lizzie, now that I lay here on this bed, to think of all the tricks and mischief I set about just a short while ago."

"Oh, you mustn't," began his sister, but he interrupted her.

"Why ever not, Lizzie, " he responded, "for ...."

And then he stopped and turned his face to the wall. He did remember with great shame the sorrow he had caused his parents who had been so eager for him to go to school. If his eyes had not been painfully oozing, he might well weep like an unbreeched boy for he felt so miserable.

"Tom," Lizzie's voice was soft. "Tom, you have been such a grand brother to me always."

Tom swallowed audibly.

"John Hooper," he went on, his voice shaking a trifle, "is such a man as I would like to be. Perhaps I shall be a preacher, Lizzie. For surely people can be blind and still preach."

The girl smiled. Although she had great sympathy for her brother, she could not for the life of her picture him as a preacher.

"I know you are smiling," the boy said, "I can sense it, you minx of a sister! But I mean it. I have done with wasting time. I will ask Master Philip to school me more and more in Bible knowledge. And I also want to go and hear John Hooper preach. Master Philip has told me that at his home there is a table spread in the common hall with a good store of meat. It is daily beset of beggars and poor folk. Every day John Hooper eats with a certain number of poor folk, Lizzie. Is that not a great thing to do?"

The girl nodded, but then remembering that her brother could not hear a nod, spoke.

"Yes, Tom."

"He also questions the poor folk at his table as to whether they know the Lord's prayer, and the Ten Commandments, and what they believe. And after this he sits down with them and eats."

"He sounds like a good man, Tom."

"Yes," her brother agreed, repeating, "and when I am better, Lizzie, you shall take me to hear him preach. I think he preaches in the cathedral and also betimes on the street."

It took the greater part of a year for Tom to fully recuperate. Afterwards he walked about with a cane - tapping out the space before him - amazing himself that he was able to recall the steps, the ruts, the holes, the sights and sounds of the farm and thus ascertain where he was. After a few weeks, he ventured into Gloucester. At first Lizzie guided him. Later his mother accompanied him into town, or he would venture with Philip for a stroll into the country. The lessons continued. The boy had grown in wisdom as he lay on his sickbed, drinking in the tinker's instruction with a great thirst.

"Why did you not become a preacher, Master Philip?" he questioned his tutor one day as they were strolling.

"I don't know," the man answered honestly, "but I do think that God has used me to sell Bibles and to explain certain matters about Scripture to all sorts of country folk as I traveled the roads. These were good things to do and I think that God required it of me. God has tasked me with various matters over the years and right now, methinks, he has tasked me with you, Tom."

"Well, I am glad," the boy replied, and then, switching the topic, "I have heard tell in town that King Edward is ill with a fever. Have you heard this also, Master Philip?"

"Yes, I have," the tinker answered gravely, "and I fear it is common knowledge that our young and good monarch is dying. It is also said that there is a plot afoot to put his eldest sister Mary on the throne to succeed him."

"Mary?"

"Yes, and I fear that she would return the country to papistry."

"What would that mean, Master Philip?"

"You know what that would mean, Tom. It would mean that all the things I have taught you over the past year would be condemned as heresy."

The boy stood still. He seemed dazed.

"Tell me more."

The tinker saw that the lad's face was serious.

"Well, Tom, images and relics would come back; people would be encouraged to kneel to a piece of bread at Mass; and they would be told to confess their sins to a priest rather than to God Himself."

Phlox were blooming alongside the path. It's perfume was a sugary, sweet scent and Tom recognized it. The smell vividly brought to mind the color pink that they were. Alongside their smell, he could detect the faint odor of carrot and knew that the white and delicate Queen Anne's lace, could not be too far off. Queen Anne's lace was more commonly called bishop's weed. Perhaps, Tom thought, if Bishop Hooper had been a plant, he might not have minded wearing Queen Anne's lace. And then he grinned to himself.

In the year that followed, Thomas grew more and more accustomed to walking the roads. History surrounded him as he walked and tapped the cane in front of him. Edward VI died; the brief ten day reign of Lady Jane Grey followed; and then Parliament, having restored her right of succession, aided Mary to the throne. The Six Articles were reinstated and the citizens of Gloucester learned that their beloved Bishop Hooper had been imprisoned by the new queen. But just before this occurred, to the dismay and horror of the entire Drourie family, Tom was taken into custody. He was thirteen years of age.

Thomas' arrest happened quite suddenly. Walking across Westgate Bridge one early morning, carefully tapping out his steps, he met his father's old nemesis, Father Serly. Father Serly, still short and stout, had survived Edward's reign by outwardly conforming to Protestantism. However, as soon as Mary ascended the throne and papist rules made a comeback, he emerged ready to wage war on anyone who was not attending Mass.

"Thomas Drourie," he called out, as the blind boy was about to pass by him.

Thomas stopped, recognized the priest's voice, but answered nothing.

"I have not seen you at Mass of late," Father Serly went on, using the very same words he had spoken to the boy's father seventeen years past.

"No," Tom agreed.

"Have you been ill? Has there been no one who could guide you?"

The words were friendly enough, but there was underlying threat. Tom perceived it. His father made no secret of the fact that he disliked Father Serly and a great many of the other priests. He was also fully aware that the Cathedral had reverted back to papistry and that many Protestant Englishmen had fled England.

"Well, Tom?"

As the boy still did not answer, the priest assumed that perhaps the lad did not know it was a priest he was speaking with.

"I am your Father," he said, somewhat loftily.

"I have only one Father," Tom then replied, "and He is in heaven."

"Are you being rude, young sir?"

But Tom stood quiet again, and there was no sound but the water of the Big Severn rushing underneath the bridge. Deciding not to continue in conversation with the priest, he began tapping out his steps again, walking forward as he did so. The short but stout cleric blocked his path.

"I asked you a question, young Tom Drourie."

The boy laughed and pushed at the black robes which prevented his continuing on towards Gloucester. He was young and blind, but he was strong and his shove succeeded in thrusting the priest against the side of the bridge. Not only that, but the unexpected motion caused the friar to fall face down on the slats amid the laughter of some local folk crossing over from the other side. Humiliated, the priest later complained to the town guard with the result that Tom was forcibly taken from his home later that evening into the custody of a soldier for an overnight imprisonment. His father had to pay a hefty fine the next morning to have the boy released.

"You must not be so bold, Tom"

Lizzie was sitting on a bale of hay next to her brother.

"You could get father and mother into trouble by such behavior. You would not want that."

Her brother shook his head.

"No, of course I would not."

"Well, then, you must stay at home and if you want something, either I or Albert will go with you into town."

"Philip has told me that Master Hooper was arrested, Lizzie. He is being kept in Fleet Prison in London."

"Yes, that is true."

The girl spoke softly, knowing that Tom looked up to the man, admired him and would feel badly about the news.

"He probably," Tom went on, "has no family who can set bail for him as I have heard that his wife and children have left England. The queen, Philip said, wants him dead."

"Oh."

It was all that Lizzie could think of to say. She was seventeen now and a beauty with long brown hair, just like her mother. She and Albert now had an agreement between the two of them. He had of late, spoken with her father. For a moment she forgot the young brother sitting next to her on a bale of hay. Albert was almost thirty now and she knew that during the conversation he'd had with father he had not been refused. Father had carefully weighed the facts. These were that Tom would never be able to run the farm on his own; that Albert was an honest man who truly loved her; and that Albert also truly cared for Tom. She glanced at the boy sitting next to her. He was staring straight ahead. But surely he must be staring at something within himself, for his eyes could see nothing in the barn. Albert often took him ploughing in the fields, had him walk by his side, explained what he was doing, and always included him in conversations about planting, harvesting, and caring for the cattle. Could they not all live in harmony - father, mother, Albert and herself - protecting and keeping Tom and the farm?

"They say," Tom interrupted her thoughts, and speaking vehemently, "that those who put Bishop Hooper in prison accuse him of owing the queen money. But it is not true! They are lying about him!"

"Hush, Tom! Do not take on so."

Lizzie put her right arm about Tom's shoulder as she spoke. But Tom went on, his hands striking the air in anger.

"The real reason, Lizzie, is that they want him dead! They want him dead because he is a Protestant just like we are."

Tom's last words sounded flat and hollow. She was slightly alarmed at them.

"The heresy acts have been revived," Tom continued, his voice somber.

"We just have to stay on the farm, Tom," Lizzie answered, "We won't get involved. Father and mother don't go into Gloucester very much anymore and we have all we need right here."

"There is a rumor, but I think it is the truth," the boy went on, "that Bishop Hooper will be transferred to Gloucester at some point. When he is, I want you to take me to his place of confinement, Lizzie. Will you promise me that you will?"

Lizzie did not answer.

"Well, if you will not take me, then I shall ask Master Philip or Albert."

"No, not Albert."

Lizzie's answer was swift now.

"Well, then?"

"Yes, Tom. If and when Master Hooper comes back to Gloucester, I shall take you to see him, if that is possible."

Satisfied, the boy leaned into her shoulder.

"You are a good sister, Lizzie."

Approximately two months later, in February of 1555, word came to the citizens of Gloucester that their former bishop, John Hooper, would be taken, under heavy escort, to Gloucester. It was Philip the tinker who recounted this to the Drouries at noon.

"Actually," he went on, glancing at Tom's white face as he spoke, "he was taken to Gloucester today. Although the news of his coming was kept secret, it leaked out. A mile outside town, I saw vast crowds assembled - men and women all crying and lamenting Hooper's sorry state as he passed."

"You were there? You saw him?" Tom asked.

"Yes, I did, Tom. I watched as one of the queen's guards, and there were six of them for the one man, rode into Gloucester to ask for the aid of the mayor and sheriffs. These namby-pamby guards were worried that Hooper would be rescued by the hosts of people standing at the side of the road hailing their former pastor. Then I saw a great many officers armed with weapons come to the North Gate. They ordered the people to go home and to stay home and then conducted John Hooper to a place where he will be kept until.... "

He left off and it was quiet.

"Until what?" Tom finally threw out.

"Until his burning at the stake tomorrow."

There was quiet around the table. Lizzie, who sat across from Tom, felt his foot kick her shin. She winced slightly, but she knew what it meant.

They managed to leave the farm together under the pretext of visiting one of Lizzie's friends.

"I don't know where to take you, Tom, for Philip did not say where they lodged the bishop."

"You must take me to the Cathedral then, Lizzie. For at that place they will know of a certainty where he has been taken."

"Even so, Tom, why should they tell you."

"Because they will."

"Well, I will take you. But you must promise me to be careful."

The boy did not answer and they walked along in silence, the boy tapping his path all the while, his cane in his right hand and Lizzie holding his left.

When they arrived at the Cathedral, the Gloucester streets were eerily quiet. People had been ordered to stay indoors.

"Take me to a side door, Lizzie, and I will knock. You need not stay. But do not go too far either."

Lizzie squeezed his hand in response and brought him to a nether door. The boy began knocking almost before she had time to find her way around a corner. Tom pounded loudly and persistently and at the beginning no one came to answer. But he continued in fervor, scraping his knuckles on the wood. At length a guard opened the door.

"What do you want, lad?"

His voice was not unfriendly and Tom took heart.

"I want to see Bishop Hooper."

The guard was taken aback for he could see that Tom was blind.

"Please sir," Tom repeated, "let me speak with the Bishop. I much desire to hear his last words to me before he goes to the stake."

"Are you family?"

"Yes, he is to me as a father."

The guard, who was not a bad fellow, relented upon hearing the earnestness in the boy's plea.

"Very well, then, come along."

"You must give me your hand, sir."

Thomas reached out and the guard took his hand, drawing him inside the building.

"Come along then and tell me your name."

"Tom Drourie, sir."

The guard moved them along a corridor at a good pace, talking the whole while.

"My name is Edmund Wells, Tom, and it is a sad business, this whole thing, is it not? But your name sounds familiar. Was there not a boy named Tom arrested a short time ago for ...."

He stopped, scratched his head, and then smiled.

"Yes, now I remember. It had to do with Father Serly, a man I care little about. If I recall correctly, it was because this certain Tom had pushed him."

"Yes, sir."

Tom answered softly, hoping the conversation would not cost him his chance to see Bishop Hooper."

"Well, Tom, if that was you, I would not take it to heart. Father Serly is ... well, he is not overly truthful and he is much concerned about himself. But be careful what you say, boy, these are treacherous times."

Tom nodded and the guard chatted on.

"Bishop Hooper will be taken to Robert Ingram's house later today. He's not to stay in a common gaol, that good man, but in a home where they respect him. So that is a blessing. And now we have come to his cell. I must let go of your hand to open the door with my key. There's a good lad. Just stand here."

Thus speaking, the guard opened the door before returning to Tom. Reaching for his hand, he propelled him inside the small cubicle, never stopping for breath.

"Here's a young lad come to bid you good day, Master Hooper. Says his name is Tom - Tom Drourie. I believe Tom was arrested a while back as well for speaking disrespectfully to a priest. I'll collect him by and by."

With that he shut the door and Tom was alone with the bishop.

It was a small cell. Tom could feel the walls close and the ceiling low. He stepped forward hesitantly, tapping his cane carefully.

"Good afternoon, sir," he finally mumbled, his voice emerging small and thin.

"Good afternoon, Tom," he was answered by a friendly and low voice, "and what brings you to visit me here in this sad place?"

"I wished to say," Tom began, "I wished to say that I will pray for you, sir. It must be dreadfully ... dreadfully ...."

He could not go on and a moment later felt a hand on his shoulder.

"There, there lad," both Bishop Hooper's voice and hand guided him along, "Here's a chair. Sit yourself down and we shall have a talk, you and I, and find out what is in your heart."

Tom breathed in deeply, ashamed that he was blubbering like an unbreeched child again.

"Thank you, sir," he managed.

"Well, Tom," the bishop continued, putting him at his ease, "I've a lad just like you at home. Only he's left England and I don't get to see him any more. I miss him very much and so appreciate your visit for that reason alone. If I had my lad here, I would counsel him to hold fast to the faith."

"Yes, sir," Tom responded, his blind eyes unwaveringly fixed upon the place he deemed Bishop Hooper to be.

"Do you believe in the Lord Jesus, son?"

"Oh, yes, sir."

"Do you confess His one sacrifice on the cross and deny the popish idolatry in the Mass?"

"Oh, yes, sir," Tom breathed out again.

"Well, lad, then there will not be a goodbye between us once the guard comes to take you back. For of a verity, we will see one another in heaven."

"Do you think I shall see?" Tom ventured, "in heaven."

"Yes, Tom, you certainly shall."

There was a long quiet, but it was not awkward. The bishop had taken the boy's hand into his own. After a while he spoke again.

"Ah, Thomas! Ah, poor boy! God has taken from you your outward sight, for what consideration He best knows. But He has given you another sight much more precious, for He has induced your soul with the eye of knowledge and faith. God give you grace continually to pray to Him that you lose not that sight, for then you should be blind both in body and soul."

Tom nodded, his eyes again filling with tears. At that moment the door opened with a groan of heaviness and disuse.

"Tom, time to go."

It was Edmund, the guard, and Tom stood up. The bishop clapped him on the shoulder.

"Son, may God bless you and keep you and let His face shine upon you and be gracious unto you."

Taking Tom's hand, the guard steered him through the door into the hall and all the while Tom was mindful how the lark had sung in the field where he had been with Philip; and he recalled with great clarity how the bull had charged and how Philip had played the viol.

Walking back towards the entrance, Tom begged Edmund for permission to hear Bishop Hooper speak to the people of Gloucester prior to his being burned at the stake. For so it was that condemned men were allowed to address the crowd before being martyred. Without a word, the man took the boy through to another anteroom, one that led into the cathedral. Although Tom could not see it, this was where Dr. Williams, the Chancellor of Gloucester, was sitting behind a desk. The registrar sat next to him and they were concentrating on some paperwork. Without waiting for permission, the guard addressed them.

"Begging your pardon for disturbing you as you work by the sanctuary, your Honour, but this boy wants permission to hear the bishop speak tomorrow before his martyrdom."

"Martyrdom, Wells?

"Whatever it pleases your Honour to call it," the man answered, before he abruptly turned about and left, abandoning Tom in the sanctuary.

Dr. Williams, who was a heavy-set man, turned from the paperwork to peer at Tom.

"What is your name, boy?"

"Thomas Drourie, sir."

"And you wish to see Bishop Hooper die?"

"Not die, sir, but live."

"Are you a good Christian, Tom?"

"I try to be, sir."

"Hmmh," the chancellor said, and glancing at the registrar added, "Well, suppose we ask you some questions as to ascertain that."

Tom stood in front of him, cane in hand, eyes fixed on where the chancellor's voice came from.

"Do you believe," the chancellor began, "that after the words of the priest's consecration, the very body of Christ is in the bread?"

Tom responded strongly with a very loud, "No, that I do not!"

Dr. Williams looked keenly at the disabled boy in front of him.

"Then you are a heretic, Thomas Drourie. Do you know that for this reason alone you can be burned? Who taught you this heresy?"

Tom, the eyes of his heart bright, even though his outward sight was dull, answered clearly, "You, Mr. Chancellor."

Dr. Williams sat up straight.

"Where I pray you."

The words echoed hollowly through the sanctuary.

Tom replied softly but clearly, pointing with his cane towards the place where he supposed the pulpit was, "In yonder place."

Dr. Williams was aghast.

"When did I teach you so?"

Tom, now looking straight at where the chancellor's voice was coming from, replied plainly and distinctly: "When you preached a sermon to all men, as well as to me, upon the sacrament. You said the sacrament was to be received spiritually by faith, and not carnally and really as the papists have heretofore taught."

Dr. Williams looked down at the papers in front of him. He felt a certain shame flood his heart. Nevertheless his voice boomed out and resounded in the aisles.

"Then do as I have done, and you shall live as I do and escape burning."

Aware that the bull was charging, but hearing the viol, Tom answered calmly and firmly: "Though you have easily dispensed with your own self and mock God, the world and your conscience, I will not do so."

Dr. Williams was vexed, vexed in his soul. Although he tried for some time to convince the boy otherwise, threatening him plenty, there was no recantation.

Finally he bellowed: "Then God have mercy upon you, Tom, for I will read you your condemnatory sentence."

Tom answered, "God's will be fulfilled."

At this moment the registrar nudged Dr. Williams.

"For shame, man! Will you read the sentence and condemn yourself? Away with you! At least substitute someone else to give sentence and judgment."

But Dr. Williams would not change his mind.

"Mr. Registrar!" he barked out, "I will obey the law and give sentence myself according to my office."

After this he read Tom his death sentence, albeit with a discomfited tongue and a twisted conscience.

"Wells," he then cried out, for the guard had re-entered the sanctuary, "take this boy to a cell."

"Sir, I beg you," a small voice cried out in the back of the sanctuary, "have mercy on my brother."

It was Lizzie who had been allowed into the cathedral by the kindhearted Edmund.

"Do you wish to be arrested alongside your brother?"

"Sir, I would fain take his place if it would help his case."

Tom felt love well up in his heart for his sister. Often she had kept him from wrongdoing in the past; often she had nursed scraped elbows and bruises; and often she had comforted him when he had been lonely. She was like a second mother. Ah, his mother! Tears sprung to his eyes. He had not thought of his parents this whole time. Lizzie slowly lifted one foot in front of the other, as if she were gathering courage in those unhurried steps. Reaching the front, she stood straight before Dr. Williams.

"He is but a lad, your honor," she haltingly began, "and his mother ...."

Then she wept. Tom was at her side in an instant.

"Don't cry, Lizzie," he pleaded, "please don't cry."

"How can I help it Tom?"

"You will see me again, Lizzie."

She lifted her tearstained face towards him, doubtful and hopeful at the same time.

"Tell mother and father that I shall be home shortly, Lizzie. And tell them that I look forward to that homecoming more than anything else."

Then Edmund Wells took the boy's hand in his own and led him away.

****

A true story, flavored with fiction, the blind boy, Thomas Drourie, (together with a bricklayer by the name of Thomas Croker), was burned at the stake on May 5, 1556. This was three months after Bishop Hooper was burned. Three years later, during the early years of Queen Elizabeth's reign, Chancellor Williams poisoned himself thus adding suicide to his previous crimes. For Thomas Drourie, Bishop Hooper and other faithful believers, there was the cover of Jesus' blood and the light of God's countenance; for Chancellor Williams, what shall we say?

The Corner of His Garment

When I passed by you again and saw you, behold, you were at the age for love, and I spread the corner of my garment over you and covered your nakedness; I made my vow to you and entered into a covenant with you, declares the Lord GOD, and you became mine (Ezekiel 16:8).

The summer of 1665 began and ended with extraordinary heat. The preceding spring and winter had been extremely dry, drier actually than anyone living could remember. The cloudless sky shimmered, meadows hazed and soil crumbled to the touch. Yet, though spindly, corn grew, and fruit trees bore fruit. In all apparent barrenness, persistent roots drew up supplies of water from hidden reservoirs below the earth.

David Baxter sweated copiously on his second day of travel towards London. The road was hard beneath his feet and betimes he stumbled over rocky lumps of earth and clay with less dignity than he would have liked. The great houses or manors he passed every now and then seemed deserted. Lengthy lanes with pollarded trees and pleached branches and vines, lay eerily still. Ponds and distant terraces echoed no sounds safe the trebling of some birds. And even these few birds seemed mostly of a disposition not to sing. David did not wonder unduly at the silence. He surmised that people had left their estates to travel elsewhere as he had heard from people he met on the road that the plague was once again wreaking havoc in London and he was only an hour or so within walking distance of that city. He did not fear or dwell on the news. After all, the plague always seemed to be somewhere, like the ebb and tide of the sea, coming and going, taking and leaving.

Stallworth, the hamlet from which David hailed, was but a small place and not privy to much news. A tiny community, many miles northeast of London, it was nestled between woodlands and hills and bordered a small Thames tributary. Composed of some two hundred villagers, the greater part of whom were Puritans, they did not hold with monarchy. The occasional tales that reached their ears of the restored monarch's libertine nature, had turned sour and cynical whatever regard they might have had for the king.

Jesse Baxter, David Baxter's father, was the preacher of Stallworth. He had been given a certificate of preaching some ten years previous by the triers, a board of commissioners established by Oliver Cromwell. Jesse Baxter had received the rectory of Stallworth in 1655 when David was but ten years old. He preached a truthful doctrine, prayed with passion, administered the Lord's Supper, visited the sick and also cultivated glebe lands. The Stallworth folk loved him. Jesse did not think it beneath himself to work, to get his hands dirty. He understood the feel and texture of the soil, what crops were best suited to it and he delighted in the woods around Stallworth.

Cromwell was now both dead and buried, but the Stallworth church continued with many Puritan practices. Even though the people prayed faithfully every Sunday for a change of heart in their lecherous king, they had little faith in his actual conversion. High upon a brass in the small country church were written these words:

Why glory in the splendor of thy race? It fades apace.
Why glory in illustrious descent? It came and went.

When word reached Stallworth that it had been mandated that every minister should publicly declare his assent to everything in the Book of Common Prayer or lose his benefice, Jesse Baxter simply shrugged and went on preaching, planting, living and teaching his congregation. Many of his colleagues, pious and learned men of irreproachable life, lost their pulpits. But Jesse Baxter, in the tiny, almost forgotten hamlet of Stallworth, stayed on.

David reflected on all this as he passed through the fields of Islington and approached London. He loved, respected and obeyed his father in all things but wondered whether Stallworth was not too isolated in these matters. There were friends and relatives who had died in Newgate Prison, who had paid a price for their faith. His father, although speaking up publicly in Stallworth, had never been faced with imprisonment, simply because no one was aware of his dissent. He could hardly imagine his father in the pillory, much as he tried. Stallworth was not a well-known place. David doubted sincerely whether its existence was known to the rest of England, or for that matter, whether the good people of Stallworth, besides the fact that they despised the king, knew much else about their fair country. But if he himself, David Baxter, were faced with a difficult decision, a decision that might force him into danger, would he be able to make the right one.

It was getting close to dusk when David walked into London through Moorgate. He marveled at the strange stillness of its smoky breath. The stink of the emptied slop-pails, the absence of jabbering peddlers, and the foulness of the air all devoid of people at this still relatively early evening hour, made him uneasy. After turning onto Throckmorton Street, on which Brown Horse Inn was located, he paused to get his bearings. The quiet continued, except that church bells rang intermittently. The few people he did pass, seemed strangely subdued and most walked in the middle of the road, neither on one side or on the other. Reaching the inn, he was surprised to see that its shutters were down. About to knock, David noted a paper tacked to the wall. Moving closer so he could decipher its message in the approaching darkness, he read: "This is to notify all customers that I, John Barhouse, have dismissed my servants and shut up my Inn, for so long as this Scourge will last, intending, (God willing), to return Michaelmas next, so that all persons whatsoever who have any accompts with me, can deal with me at that time."

"Hey, there! You lad."

A group of men walking alongside a horse-drawn cart were making their way up Throckmorton Street. David looking about and seeing no one else, realized that they were beckoning him. Past the clanging and the clapping of the church bells they called again.

"Hey, you there! Come here."

He stepped towards them, observing for the first time the red crosses in the middle of the doors of several houses adjacent to the inn. The words '*Lord, have Mercy upon us*' were clearly marked out next to the crosses. The bells stopped and the sound of the cart wheels turning harshly over the dry ground touched his ears gratingly. The men, there were four of them, did not appear menacing. He judged them to be in their thirties. Reaching the group, he stopped walking. But he was both alarmed and filled with dread when he saw that the cart at their side was filled with bodies, bodies wrapped up in cloths, rugs and sheets.

"Where be you going, lad?"

The first of the men spoke, though not unkindly. When David did not answer, for indeed the shock of the moment held him in its grip, he went on.

"The curfew of nine o'clock is close. You can be fined by the sheriff if seen loitering about. Are you looking for relatives, lad?"

David shook his head and spoke, clearing his throat as he did so. He could not take his eyes off the corpses in the cart.

"I'm supposed to stay at the inn overnight, but I see that it is closed."

He stopped short.

"You're not from London then and you may not know that the plague has visited this city for the last few months with a vengeance."

David shook his head again but even as he shook it, a woman came out of the house behind him. Wagging her finger at the men, her voice overrode the bells which had begun again.

"You took your time boys. There's quite a haul in here. Move then! Be quick about it! Take them out! Take them out!"

All four men were smoking pipes and after tugging at them vigorously, left their places by the cart and walked past the woman. She stood aside, watching them enter the house. David was numb with trepidation. He could not move and began to tremble. The woman regarded him with some curiosity.

"Are you seized with the illness?"

The bells stopped once more as two of the men came back out onto the street. They carried a corpse. The woman moved next to David. He stared at the body and she sang, softly under her breath:

Ring a-ring a-Roses
A pocketful of posies,
'Tishoo, 'tishoo,
We all fall down!

In quick succession the men carried the bodies out to the cart. Some were wrapped in sheets; some in rugs. Hands on her hips, the woman surveyed the trips they made with some satisfaction and remarked to David that she would receive four-pence each for the bodies she had discovered. He did not reply but, trying to control his shaking, eyed the cart. Those in it short days ago had breathed, sung, and loved and were now gone forever.

"He was a barber, name of John Block," the woman offered.

Her hands came down from her hips and she wiped them on her apron.

"He thought the plague had abated somewhat, I take it. Took to interpreting the Bill of Mortality too favorably, I don't doubt. It was down a bit for the last two weeks, you see. He'd gone to Rochester with his whole family to visit a brother. Locked up this house and left. But then he up and came back. Perhaps the brother was tired of feeding him and his."

She stopped and moved aside as another body was carried out. It was a child, no more than three or four years old. The little head lolled unsupported out of a sheet.

"John Block had five children," the woman went on, "five sons, for boys they all were. He had two apprentices and a maid-servant for his wife as well. Doing well, I'd say, he was. But he'd only been back less than a week when the distemper broke out in his own family. That was last week. And within five days, the same number as his sons, you see, they all died. Himself, his wife, his sons, his maid-servant and his apprentices. All dead."

She wiped her hands again and David watched as the men straightened the bodies on the cart. The little boy neat as a mummy, rolled against his dead mother. He swallowed audibly.

"Where you from, boy?"

It was the man who had spoken to him at the first.

"From Stallworth."

The man shook his head, indicating he had never heard of the place.

"What are you about then?"

The man spoke gruffly but not unkindly.

"I'm to deliver a letter from my father to Sir Christopher Morton in Throckmorton Street. I was to sleep in the inn here and deliver it in the morning."

"Well, lad, there's no sleeping in these quarters. And as for your Sir Christopher, he's left London - he as well as a great many other gentry folk."

As David's face registered a certain amount of helplessness, the man kindly continued.

"Why don't you come with me. I think I can put you up for the night. But then you must first follow me to complete this business. We could use a hand."

David shuddered and was about to answer negatively. But the sweet face of the boy who slept by his mother in the wagon withheld him. Someone had to bury these people. Were they not all creatures of God?

The woman disappeared ahead of the cart carrying a red rod some three feet in length. He had not noted it before and concluded that perhaps she had kept it hidden under her apron. Cautiously David fell in next to the man who had spoken to him. Up to this point none of the other men had said a word to him or to one another.

"You did not know London had the plague?"

"No, that is, I heard rumors as I traveled but did not know that it was so bad."

"It is a dreadful thing!"

They walked silently for a spell and then David ventured a question.

"Where are we going?"

"Aldgate. To the great Pit in the churchyard of our Parish of Aldgate. It is a terrible and deep Pit. So deep that they who dug it hit water and could dig no deeper."

David could think of no reply and did not relish the thought of coming to the Pit. Trudging alongside the men in silence, he spoke no more and every minute or so the leading man would ring his bell, clanging it alongside the noise of the great church bells.

After almost half an hour of steady trudging the small group of buriers reached the churchyard at Aldgate. The bellman rang loudly and the sexton, who appeared at the gate, waved them on. There were several other carts there as well but they had already done their awful business and passed by them back onto the street. David stood stopped walking. He was uncertain. There was enough daylight left so that he could see the Pit. The cart had been drawn clear up to its mouth. A shovel was put into his hands and he was instructed to throw dirt on the bodies as soon as they fell from the cart. This he did. Some of the coverings on the corpses came off as they were heaved from the cart and they fell quite naked into the hole. Huddled together in a common grave they knew not that they were naked. And because he had to hold on to something or he would be violently ill, David began to pray. Words tumbled off his lips, words such as he had heard his father pray at grave sides, but never a grave such as this.

"Thou, O Lord, art mighty in heaven. Thou art indeed, the Creator of Heaven and Earth. What is man that Thou art mindful of him and the son of man, that Thou shouldst visit him? He is frail, made of dust and to dust he returns. He is not a man but a worm. But it is in Thee that we live and move and have our being. It is in Thee only that our Hope lies."

Unconsciously, as he shoveled the dirt onto the poor, undignified bodies, David's voice had grown louder and louder. He did not note that the other men had stopped working and were listening to him with something akin to amazement.

"Unto Thee will I cry, O Lord, my rock; be not silent to me: lest, if Thou be silent to me, I become like them that go down into the pit. Hear the voice of my supplications, when I cry unto Thee, when I lift up my hands towards Thy holy oracle."

He stopped and leaned on his shovel, wiping his face with the edge of his sleeve.

"You are a parson?"

It was the bell ringer who spoke. David moved away from the Pit.

"No," he said, his voice breaking, "But I hope to be."

****

Robert Heath, for that was the name of the man who had spoken kindly to him, took David to his quarters. These quarters were strange indeed as they turned out to be a small wherry docked on the Thames.

"I can offer you no food tonight, lad, but tomorrow it might be that we can find some victuals by the market. There are still many who come to sell."

It was a balmy night but such was the stink of the city and such was the clarity of David's remembrance of the corpses, that he found it hard to breathe. He sorely missed his home. He wondered what his mother and father would think when they became aware that the plague was raging so. He arranged his cloak as pillow and tried to obliterate from his mind all that had happened to him this last half day. Yet such was the constitution of his young frame that he slept almost immediately with a prayer on his lips: "I will both lay me down in peace, and sleep: for Thou, Lord, only makest me dwell in safety."

It was early morning when David woke. He yawned, stretched and it took only a moment for him to realize where he was. Slowly he sat up, taking in his surroundings. There were many boats around the wherry - boats covered with tilts, bales and furnished with straw for comfort. They lay by the shore, some having used their sails to put up little tents alongside the Thames. Robert Heath as yet sat snoring. David studied at the man who had been so kind as to take him along. Heath looked to be his father's age but was thinner, had red hair and gave the impression of being covered with weariness.

There was a stirring in one of the boats moored nearby. A child whimpered and some seagulls cried out overhead. Robert stirred and opened his eyes, a pained expression falling across his face. He coughed, then eased himself up out of the half-lying, half-sitting position in which he had been.

"You sleep well, lad?"

"Yes."

Robert stretched his arms and his legs as much as the wherry would permit. Then, carefully standing up, he lifted a sack from the prow and stepped ashore. David, not knowing what else to do, followed his example. Silently the pair of them walked along the sea wall of the Thames. Presently, to their left, they came within view of some houses, all boarded up.

"Here David," Robert said, stopping and pointing, "are many desolate houses where almost all are sick or dead."

He plodded on for a few moments and then pointed again, this time to a small, wooden structure, also boarded up. It had been painted green at some pleasant hour in the past and although not freshly coated, was somewhat cheerier in appearance than the surrounding houses.

"It has pleased Almighty God," said Robert, "to visit my family as well. This is where my wife and three children live."

"They have the plague?" Robert asked, horrified that Robert should walk by his own home in what seemed to be a morning stroll of sorts.

"My poor wife and three little ones still live," Robert said.

Then he left off both the walking and the speaking. Stopping as well and looking at his companion David noted that tears were coursing down Robert's cheeks.

"Why are you not in the house with them," he could not help exclaiming, "Why are you out here? Have you abandoned them?"

"I was not in when the two other children died," Robert answered, all the while looking across at the little dwelling. "And this was God's mercy, for who would provide food for my family except myself. I am a waterman by day and a burier by night, and as such I can presently eke out a living by fetching things for the larger boats on the Thames. These boats are used as shelters for other families - families which have closed themselves off for fear of infection."

He turned and pointed to the larger vessels lying at anchor.

"I fetch provisions for them," Robert continued, "by rowing up to both Greenwich and Woolwich. I go to the single farm houses where I am known and buy eggs, chickens and butter. I bring these and additional things such as I can get to the people on the boats and they pay me. And from this I can provide for my little family, provide as long as God wills."

His voice broke, and the burly man wept. David was embarrassed, but also wished he could help in some way. A few moments later, Robert recovered himself and, straightening his back, hallooed across the distance towards the little house that held his loved ones. There was, a few moments later, an answering call and a women put her head out a casement window. She waved and made signs to her husband that she would come out soon.

"Our son," Robert said, "had a swelling yesterday. But it broke and I am hoping that he may recover. This betimes happens, you know ...."

He stopped abruptly, turning to face the river. The early light of dawn revealed more people up and about by the boats. They moved quietly and for all the number of them, there was very little noise. It was as if they were afraid that making noise would bring death. Robert picked up the sack he had placed next to him and moved closer to the house. There was a large basket near the door and in this basket he emptied the sack. It contained some bread, some salt fish and a casket of beer. He arranged all of the viands neatly in the basket, his hands lingering over the food as if by doing so he was touching his family. Then, walking back to the embankment, he stood waiting. Presently the door opened and Robert's wife walked out together with a little girl, a toddler. They picked up the food, waved to Robert and turned to go back inside. But the little girl began to cry out at the sight of her father and her mother had to restrain her or she would have run across the way to meet him.

"The Lord keep you all," Robert bellowed to them before he turned to go back. David followed. He knew not what to say.

There was a woman waiting for them at Robert's wherry, the same woman who had been with the burying group the previous night. Wasting no time with niceties, she addressed David directly.

"I heard that you were a preacher. Is that true?"

"What do you want, Kate?"

It was Robert who answered her and who placed himself between David and her person.

"I want to know, is the young lad a church-going lad? I've somewhat to ask him."

"What do you want to ask me?"

David was leery of the woman. He neither liked nor trusted her but did not know why. Perhaps because she had told him that she was being paid for discovering the dead. Perhaps because she had sung a meaningless ditty while the bodies were being carried out. He did not know.

"I want to ask you to put Christian charity into deed."

She paused and sidled closer to him, lowering her voice a few decibels.

"I know of a young child, a girl, who is shut up, locked up as it were, in a house where she has neither chance nor desire to live. I would ask you, sir, to come with me and to help this child escape the bonds of sure death."

She paused for breath and Robert again intervened.

"Kate, you know as well as I do that this is not legal. That it's not permitted...."

"Hush up, man! What do you know of it? This child, such a beautiful child too, is not meant for the distemper. She is clean and of a certainty, if she stays where she is, she will die sooner or later. Have you no compassion, man?! Have you no feelings?!"

David thought of the tears which had run down Robert's cheeks but minutes ago and wondered if Kate knew about his family.

"I will go with you," he suddenly volunteered.

Robert shook his head.

"I would not do it, David," he interposed. "There are many children and," here he glanced rather vindictively at Kate, "God, in His infinite mercy, knows Whom He will spare and Whom He will not spare."

"But we might help mercy along a little, mightn't we?"

Kate laughed coarsely at her own joke and then stopped, narrowly fixing her gaze on David. Under her intense scrutiny, David recalled his thoughts of the previous day - the time he had wondered whether his father would stand up under pressure or whether he himself, when faced with a difficult decision regarding his own safety, would be up to making sacrifices.

"I will go with Kate," he repeated to Robert.

Kate immediately turned.

"Follow me," she ordered and was up and away from the sea wall, moving fast towards the road.

"The lad did not eat last night and neither did he have a meal this morning," Robert called to her retreating figure. She did not turn but pulled a penny loaf out of her apron and kept on walking. David shrugged, took Robert's hand, shook it and pressed five shillings into it.

"May God keep you and your family," he said.

****

Kate led David on a tortuous hike through various streets and alleys, offering him a hump of bread en route. He took it gladly for he was very hungry.

"There are a great many doctors who have left London," Kate commented presently as they walked. She had been quiet for a long time but suddenly pointed out to David a door which, in bold letters, had written upon its face: *Here is a doctor to be let.*

"They are, in truth, deserters," she went on, quickening her pace, adding under her breath, "and wretched cowards."

They paced on for some time before she looked up at him, renewing conversation.

"A great many clergy left London as well. What say you to that?"

"I don't know what to say," David responded. "They perhaps had families to care for... or other matters pressing."

"A fine silly answer that is, young David! In truth when they come back, who will listen to their homilies? Who will, indeed!! And what Gospel do you pretend to preach?"

She did not give him opportunity to answer. Her polemic was filled with bitterness and anger. Her vindictive sentences and thoughts ran like lava erupting from a volcano.

"Was your Jesus afraid of lepers? I hear He was not. Did your Jesus heal? I hear that He did. Did your Jesus weep? It is said that He did. Well, your Jesus should come to London today. Many lepers, much work and weeping aplenty."

It was true that London was filled with tears. The sound of weeping fell upon them from many quarters. Heart-rending sobs of men, women and children rained through open casements. On five occasions David and Kate passed corpses on the curb. The first time David paused, uncertain as to what to do, but Kate took his arm and pulled him along.

"The buriers will come with their hand-carts," she said and that was the end of the matter.

He turned and looked at the bodies left behind and, for the first time in his life, felt the inclination to despair.

"The house we go to," Kate said presently, "is one that has been shut up."

She glanced up at him to see if he comprehended the meaning of her words. He shook his head indicating he did not understand.

"If a person is found to be sick of the plague, he is expected to stay in his house. Even if he is found to be ill with another disorder, his house will remain shut up for a month. If anyone visits him either willingly or unknowingly, it does not matter which, that person will be shut up for a certain number of days as well. No one can enter or leave the house, by order of the Lord Mayor of London himself, unless it be to the pest-house."

"Why is it," David asked, "that you could enter a house yesterday, that house where the family of ten people died, and were free to leave?"

"Because I am a searcher. This means," she continued, seeing the blank look on his face, "that I have sworn to make due search for the dead and that physicians may call on me to look through neighborhoods so that I can report who has died."

"What is to prevent people who are shut up," David asked, "to leave their houses and to go elsewhere?"

"There are watchmen," Kate answered, "watchmen with halberds. And these watchmen guard houses both night and day. They take special care that no person can enter or leave a house. It is also their duty to go for food and other things from time to time if the people in the house have need."

A half an hour later Kate and David had set foot in a wealthier neighborhood. Across from a rather imposing house, Kate finally stood still, drawing David to the side. A watchman stood by the door. Lowering her voice, Kate began to speak.

"The girl in question," she said, "is a maid-servant. She is but a child and was hired to run errands and do little jobs for the lady of that house. Last week, the child told me, her mistress came home after being gone for some hours, complaining that she was not well. A quarter of an hour later she vomited, and then said she had a violent pain in the head. The child helped her to bed and was going to fetch the doctor. But the woman bade her stay and wept so piteously that Delia, for that is the child's name, stayed. And it would not have helped the woman if the child had gone for the doctor. The disease was of such a rapid nature that there was but an hour or so before the woman died."

"How did you happen to find ...?"

David left the question dangling.

"The child was known to me. She is the daughter of a friend who has also died. I promised to look out for her."

"There was no father?"

"No."

The answer was short and curt. Glancing over David could see the stocky guard yawn as he stood by the front door of the house. The red cross and the words 'Lord have mercy' cried out behind him.

"I will tell the watchman, by and by, to go and get the child some bread. He will be off and then you can do your part."

"What must I do then?"

David was not sure any more if his impetuous response to go with Kate had not been foolhardy. What if this Delia girl had contracted the plague? What if he was arrested and put into quarantine himself? What if he caught the plague? What actually was it that the Lord required of him here in this place?

"You must needs pass the house and turn sharply right at the next lane. Cut back to the right again at the first corner after that and you will reach the back of this house. There is a garden and a wall between this house and its neighboring houses. Walk through the garden towards the house. The door you will see at the back of the house is locked but I know that the window to the right of that door is open for I tried it yesterday. Come to that window and in a short while I will hand the child to you."

Kate stopped talking and looked him full in the face. She was a shorter than he was and her face was pockmarked. She smiled at him for the first time since meeting him and although she appeared sincere in her story, he could not but sense that there were things he did not know, things she was keeping from him.

"Where shall I take the child?"

"Why, home to your people!"

She seemed much surprised at his question.

"Home?"

He repeated the answer dully, as one who did not understand. He had anticipated that his role would have been of less consequence, of less involvement.

"Yes, indeed! She cannot stay in London. There is too much danger of infection here. She would be running a risk every day. The country is much better, much safer, say you not so?" "But ...."

He found no words of response. Kate handed him a small satchel from under her apron.

"Here are some clothes for the child. She will come out to you naked."

"Naked?"

"Yes, this is law. No clothes must be carried away from any infected house. It is prohibited and safest for you and the child that way."

He took the packet from her and tried to collect his thoughts. He knew nothing about children safe that they were younger.

"Go now. Walk ahead of me. Don't hesitate or look back. Just do as I told you."

David obey. Tempted as he was to turn and look back at Kate, he did not. He also had a strong inclination to turn and run, to run far away from this strange and fearful matter, but this he also did not do. The packet burned in his fingers. He saw the watchman out of the corner of his eye as he passed the house, but the fellow was intent on some object at his feet, paying him no attention. Following Kate's instruction he arrived, without any difficulty, at the back of the house. The window in question was plain to see. A trifle high perhaps, but not too high for a body to be handed down. A warbler marked the air with a lively song little knowing, David reflected, that there was so much death around. He suddenly realized that it would be wise to open the packet and take out the clothes for it would be better for the child to immediately get dressed. Awkwardly picking at the strings, he undid them, much surprised when a dress fell out, not so much, as far as he could gauge, for a little child as for a young woman. A sky-blue bodice and dark blue kirtle flowed into his hands and a pair of brown shoes fell onto the grass. He stared at them for a bit, apprehensive of what was to come but not knowing how to disengage himself from this new future.

There was a commotion at the window. It opened and Kate's head appeared.

"Be ready to leave as soon as I hand the child down to you. I'll try to persuade the watchman to go to the bake-house to get some bread. When he has gone, I will let her down through the window."

"But ...."

She did not stop to listen to David. The casement cloth she had pulled aside to speak to him fell back and he was left speaking to no one. He picked up the brown shoes and then set them down again, neatly, one next to the other, laying the clothes on top. Then took the cloak from his back and held it in his arms like a blanket. Perhaps this would suffice as a cover. A few minutes later Kate's voice called down to him again before he had time to think things through properly.

"Come closer, lad. Step right up to the window. Reach up your arms then and I shall hand her down to you."

David came closer and closed his eyes for a moment. When he opened them again Kate had stopped talking and held to her bosom a young girl, unclothed and thin. Wide-eyed and scared looking, her arms clutched Kate's neck. With long, brown hair cascading down, she made David think of a young foal. He reached up his arms and took the stark-naked, trembling body from Kate, gently lowering her to the ground, trying to cover her with his cloak as he did so. Averting his eyes, he spoke haltingly.

"These are your clothes. Put them on and ...."

And then what? He was at a loss as to how to proceed but he did know that a great compassion had taken hold of him, that a great care for this shivering half-woman had crept into his heart.

"Be quick now, Delia. Put on your things."

Kate stood at the window and David looked up at her. She was quite imposing for she stood higher than they did. Delia needed no prodding. She was dressed in no time and stood mutely by his side. The cloak lay on the ground and he picked it up.

"Go back the way you came, David. Get out of London, lad, and be quick about it. Delia's in your care now. Your God has put her in your way. Remember that, if you should think to abandon her."

Kate leaned out of the window as she spoke. Her black waistcoat, embroidered with an impudent red thread, seemed to glower. And though her last sentence had all the markings of a saintly commandment, the way in which she uttered the words were like so much hissing. Inadvertently Delia moved closer to David. She seemed afraid of Kate. David took her hand. He replied not a word to Kate but turned around and led Delia towards the back alley from which he had come.

It was in this way that Delia and David began their journey out of London. A small breath of wind, easing the great humidity which held the city in its hot embrace, touched their cheeks. David turned north and not being completely unfamiliar with London, he found his way back towards Moorgate, the same gate through which he had come. The few constables they passed took no notice of them, for they were more concerned with people setting up house in the city then with those leaving. Dead carts rumbled past even though it was broad daylight. Delia shuddered each time she saw one and when David told her she must look away she replied that she could not.

"Why not?" he asked.

"I think perhaps that I shall lie in one soon and.. and if I know what it looks like, well then ... then perhaps I will not be so afraid."

"But you shall not lie in one."

"You do not know."

Her answer was low and mournful.

"What do I not know?"

"You are new here. You do not know how quickly people die. You see how the dead carts ride by, even now in the daytime? That is because the nights are too short in which to bury them. I have watched from my window."

"Delia, have you no knowledge of God's care?"

"I go not to church, if that is what you mean."

"No," David answered slowly, "I suppose that is not what I mean. I mean, have you no comfort within yourself that whatever happens, God has made it so and will help you?"

Delia shook her head. David was silent. He reflected that it had been somewhat easy to cover her with clothes but that to cover her with faith would be an entirely different matter. Then he chided himself for being too serious too quickly.

Although it had been a dry season, corn had grown well. For this reason corn bread was sold in abundance by vendors as David and Delia walked on. As well, there was much fruit to be had quite cheaply. Even though the plague was at its height, country people came and freely and boldly solicited their wares to all who were interested. David bought some fruit as well as some bread. Delia stared at the money he pulled out of his wallet.

"Do you like cherries?" he asked.

David wanted to please her, wanted to give her something to make her forget death. She smiled.

"Yes, and I fancy pears as well."

He bought some pears from the next farmer but cautioned her against eating too quickly. About to bite into a pear, she dropped it onto the ground when a man, but some two feet away from her, fell to the ground and died. The man's companion, an older woman, knelt down by his side, crying loudly. David would have gone to the woman's aid, but remembering the charge at his side, took Delia's hand and pulled her away.

"Come," he said, "or we will not make much headway today. We have quite a distance to travel."

She came along willingly, although she glanced back over her shoulder several times at the couple - he dead and she wailing. And the wailing followed them out of London.

"At Stallworth we have many woodlands and pastures, good pastures."

He spoke to break the silence as they walked into the countryside. She did not answer but walked along quietly. He observed her as she walked just a few feet ahead of him. Slim, dark and tallish, he would guess her to be not yet sixteen.

"How old are you?"

He asked the question to prove his estimate and was pleased when she confirmed it by answering that she was fifteen.

She did not volunteer anymore information, so he lapsed back into talking about Stallworth, about his home.

"The people of my village are farmers. But there are some who are into other trades as well. There is Jacob Heatherfield, the tailor and Bart Thoms who has a smithy and ...."

"And what do you do?"

Delia half turned. The sun glinted on her dark hair and he thought he saw the pools of the dark river which ran by Stallworth reflected in it.

"What do I do?" he repeated and studied the fields.

"Yes," she said, and turned her face away from him even as she strolled on.

"Well, I have studied to be a minister like my father who is the minister in our village."

She kicked a stone and it flew several yards in front of them.

"I've no use for parsons."

"Why ever not?"

"We'd a parson down the street from us. He was the first one to leave. Preached about the wrath of God and then left. It's always the poor ones who receive the wrath and its always the rich ones who are able to run away from it."

Delia's voice shot out like the stones she kicked into oblivion, but there was a righteous anger about her words. The further away they walked from London, the more life and aggression she seemed to be nursing back into her thin form.

"I've no doubt," David said, "that not all parsons are alike."

"Ah, if you're born a parson, that should be easy to believe."

She spat at the roadside and he let the topic be.

Around noon they came upon a little spring. Although almost dried out, it still managed a small trickle of water between some rocks. David bad Delia rest for a while and they sat down by its side.

"Be your village far away still?"

"Not so far but that we cannot reach it by dusk tomorrow evening."

They ate cornbread and washed it down with some spring water, catching it in their hands while they knelt down.

"It's pretty here."

Delia's voice was soft and she plucked at some dried grass in rock crevices.

"Have you never been away from London before?"

She shook her head and looked away.

"No, I've always lived there."

It was David's habit to thank God for his food, no matter where he was. Even now, as they sat by the spring, he wanted to do so.

"I'm going to pray."

"Why?"

She was surprised and stood up as if the suggestion might make her an accomplice to something to which she was averse.

"Because God always provides for me and so I want to thank Him for that."

"But you bought the food yourself, with your own money. I saw you."

"But God gave me the money. He provides all things for me and," he went on, "for you as well."

"He provided the plague?"

She said it scornfully and stood up, backing away from David. For a moment he was at a loss, but then answered, answered a little glibly.

"Yes, but He has also provided cleanness for you by taking you away from the foul contagion of the place in London. The air is pure here and you may breathe it."

She turned away from him and picking up a twig from the ground, broke it, throwing the pieces into the spring. He sighed knowing that this doctrine was hard indeed, the powerful doctrine of the providence of God, and he did not say any more. Bowing his head, he thanked God silently, within himself. Then he stood up and they continued their journey.

Stallworth had existed in relative obscurity for a number of generations. It was a close-knit community and several people greeted David as he and Delia walked down the main road through the village toward his home. The parsonage was on the north side of the little town. It was an unpretentious, but roomy two-story, stone house. The first floor consisted of a pantry, a kitchen, a study and a parlor as well as two small side bedrooms. The second floor had a sitting room and several more bedrooms.

As David opened the side door leading into the pantry, ushering Delia in front of him, he reflected how good it was to be back home. Walking on past the girl into the kitchen, he was greeted by three men sitting at the great oak table in the kitchen. They stood up as he entered. Delia stayed where she was and moved not a step beyond the mat by the door. Tongue-tied, she suddenly seemed very much the child again and not a woman.

"Hello, David".

"Hello."

Even as he spoke to the men, all of whom he knew, David motioned to Delia that she should come in as well. She hesitantly came forward, albeit at a snail's pace, with her eyes on the floor.

"We heard there was an outbreak of the plague visited on London. A traveling tinker from down south passed by here yesterday."

It was Bart Thoms, the smithy, who spoke and as David inclined his head in agreement to his words, he continued.

"There was talk in the village after that about your journey to London and when William Firth saw you coming over Portsman Ridge and that you came not alone ...."

He paused, looked inquiringly at the other men standing with him and when all nodded in encouragement, he continued rather hesitantly.

"There was some concern voiced about your companion. Whether or not she might be a danger to our village, if, that is, she hails from London."

David cleared his throat. He knew all three men standing in his father's kitchen.

"Where is my father?"

"Your father and mother are gone to Still's. Hawys' time has come and she is said to be poorly."

"It is true," David spoke slowly and weighed his words carefully as he spoke, "the plague is raging in London. There are thousands dead these past months and many more will, no doubt, die."

"Is the girl from London?"

Delia shifted her position and hid behind David.

"Yes, she is from London. God has put her on my path and in my care."

Bart Thoms, who appeared to be the spokesman for the group, continued.

"We know it is a good thing to care for others. Your father reads the law to us each Lord's Day. But is harboring someone who may be carrying the plague not a foolhardy thing? Can you answer me on this, David Baxter?"

David had not thought the matter through as completely as he should have. Indeed, he had felt some pride deep within himself that he had not shirked responsibility and had not refused to take the girl. But he knew that what Bart Thoms said was sensible. He answered carefully.

"The girl, her name is Delia, can stay in the malthouse until it is certain she carries nothing which will be of danger to others. I myself, as well, will stay in the house for some days to make sure that I have not contracted the disease.

Bart looked at the other men standing by the hard-backed, simple kitchen chairs. They dipped their heads in agreement. David's words seemed good to them. It remained quiet then. They stood, caps in hands, while nothing more was said. Then David understood they had no wish to pass close by Delia, so he took her hand and led her back outside.

"Wait over by the little house yonder," he said, "It is the malthouse I spoke of and will do you well enough. There is straw on the floor and I will bring you a blanket presently when the men are gone."

She went without a word, not even looking back over her shoulder. David watched her for a moment and then returned to the kitchen.

"She is gone," he said, "and I thank you for the Christian spirit of generosity you have shown in permitting her to stay."

They talked a bit of the weather and would not a rainfall be good presently and had he met many people on the road? Then they left.

It was dawn when Jesse and Elizabeth Baxter returned home. David was asleep at the great table in the kitchen when his mother and father walked in. His mother shook him, fearing something was wrong.

"David, what ails? Why are you not abed? We had not expected you back for some days."

It took David a moment to recollect himself, to recall all that had happened. Thick with sleep, his voice reassured them he was well before he recounted his story. They did not chide him for bringing Delia home. Indeed, Elizabeth immediately saw God's hand in the matter, recalling earnest prayers for a daughter.

"The child is comfortable? Perhaps I should check?"

But both David and his father dissuaded her, saying that the advice of the townfolk had been sound in that Delia should stay sequestered on her own for some time to make sure that the distemper had not been carried into Stallworth.

In spite of Jesse's and David's warnings, Elizabeth was up early the next morning and into the malthouse, where she clucked and fussed so over Delia that the girl became most timid. But it was a timidity which evaporated in the warmth of continued care. For Elizabeth coddled the child with fresh oat bread, eggs and tasty morsels from her own hand, and Althea, the house maid, was not allowed access to the malthouse. David confined himself to the barn. Given books by his father, he alternatley studied and pondered on all the matters that had happened.

Jesse and Elizabeth Baxter employed two servants, John and Althea. The couple lived in a cottage but a stone's throw away from the parsonage. Like other village folk, the Baxters brewed ale and baked bread; they churned butter and ground their own meal; they bred, fed and slaughtered their cattle and sheep; and they raised pigeons as well as poultry. Also, Jesse and David were both handy with the long gun, shooting game in the autumn, relishing the meat.

Although it was in the arts of needlework and spinning that Elizabeth, once Delia's weeks of quarantine were past, instructed the girl, she also taught her cooking, curing, preserving and distilling. Jesse himself set to help the girl understand letters as well as reading to her in the evenings. He liked her, often taking her with him as he went out in the fields, speaking to her as he would to a daughter and she listened to him as one being taught. In spite of her previous open dislike for ministers, Delia seemed to thrive under his tutelage. But she never spoke of the past. She was close-mouthed on parentage, on siblings or on what had occupied her time in London. And no one pried.

Because the Baxters were Dissenters, David had, by law, been excluded from entering any universities. It mattered little to him as he had attended an excellent academy for several seasons in London with a Dr. Mardow. The Dissenting academies, for there were a number of them, were not only cheaper than the acclaimed universities of the time, but they were also respectable. Students were held to account, and study habits were closely monitored. David had recently graduated from Dr. Mardow's academy, at which some of the leading Dissenters taught freely. He had graduated with honors but because of his youth, he was but twenty when he was done, felt too unfit and immature for a pulpit. So he had been home this last year. He helped his father in the field; he ran errands; he assisted with lambing; he read much; and he wrote fledgling sermons.

The months following Delia's arrival, David came and went: now in a neighboring parish to tutor a friend's child in Latin; now gone to a relative to deliver a letter; and at other times off to aid Stallworth's squire, Sir John Coverly, in matters pertaining to mortgaged lands. Coverly's manor house lay some three miles from the village. An honest Puritan gentleman, he faithfully attended church services each Lord's Day and all held him in great esteem.

Sir John often went hunting with the Baxters and in the early spring of 1666, Jesse, Sir John and David set out together to try their luck at shooting some pheasants. It was an extremely cold day and although they tracked and trailed far, there was no game to be had. The three men all wore a coat above and a waistcoat underneath their doublet for extra warmth. Towards dusk Jesse suggested that they return home and call it a day, but Sir John was no quitter.

"We mustn't give up, Jesse. Wasn't it but two Lord's Days ago that you spoke of perseverance with such eloquence?"

"Hunting pheasants was not what I had in mind."

Jesse smiled at his friend as he answered. They had come to the river and, covered with snow, it lay like a road before them.

"In London I've seen a dozen booths on the river. I've watched barbers shaving their customers, I've sat comfortably in tavern booths and beheld showmen erecting penny booths. These things, Jesse, were all done on the ice."

"In London, no doubt, you see many things done you would not see done here."

Jesse replied in jest. But he added a word of caution as Sir John began to test the surface of the river ice with his foot.

"I wouldn't trust the ice, Sir John."

"You were always the cautious man, Jesse. I'll wager a coach-and-six could roll across from one bank to another. Come man, I'm certain there's some game in the bushes on the other side. What say you, David?"

Having so spoken, Sir John stepped further out onto the ice and cautiously began sliding his way across. The thickness of the river ice was not uniform. Both Jesse and David knew there were thin spots and remained at the edge of the watercourse. They eyed one another uneasily as the ice cracked dangerously under Sir John's feet.

"Sir John. I think you should turn back."

David called overly loud and his voice echoed. But Coverly had been right about the game. Suddenly, on the other side, two partridge flew out from behind a bush. In his excitement at spotting the birds and consequently not looking down, Sir John tripped over a bulge in the uneven surface.

His head hit the frozen ice sheets with an ugly sound and, as he landed face down, water began to flow out of a crack. The fissure widened visibly during the next seconds as Sir John lay sprawled out, one leg at an awkward angle. He was but some six feet from the edge and Jesse immediately took off his gabardine coat. Flinging it out as far as he could, he tried to reach his friend. As the surcoat did not reach far enough, he pulled it back and began to venture out on the ice himself by holding onto the overhanging branch of a large tree. But even then the surface beneath him cracked ominously. He cast his cloak onto the shore towards David.

"David," he called out, "You must try and reach him. Your weight is less than mine, son."

But David stood transfixed, noting with horror that the ice on which Sir John lay was beginning to give way. Jesse neither reproached nor further urge his son but continued on towards Sir John, talking as he did so.

"Slide, friend! Slide towards me. You must turn towards me."

Sir John groaned but did not answer. Blood oozed from underneath his cap. Slowly and deliberately Jesse slid his feet towards Sir John. Inch by inch he moved towards his friend and even as he moved, felt his weight make the ice buckle and groan. Coverly opened his eyes and came too. He seemed not to know where he was.

"Throw the coat back to me, David."

David moved stiffly towards the cloak, picked it up and awkwardly threw it to his father, who despite the ineptness of the throw, caught the garment deftly with his left hand.

"Sir John!" Jesse's voice was insistent. "Sir John, take a hold of the coat which I will pass to you."

He slid the cloak across the ice, holding onto its edge tightly. This time it reached. Sir John, befuddled and not aware, looked at it without taking hold. Jesse stepped still further. And then, with a vengeance, the river took over. Black and cold it poured onto the ice, spilling fingers of water over Sir John's body and Jesse's feet.

"Father!!"

David wept. Jesse turned his face and gazed into his son's eyes for one second. Then his feet lost their hold on the surface and he fell, knees down, hands down, into the frigid, churning gap which had opened beneath him. And still, for an eternal second, he held onto the edge of the coat which lay dry before him stretched upon a piece of unbroken surface. Sir John began to struggle. Although his surcoat weighed him down, the shock of the water had brought him to his senses. David shouted incoherently. It was all water now and Jesse's gabardine disappeared.

"Father! Father!!"

David was frantic. The river had transformed into a swirling mass of treachery. But amazingly, Sir John had managed to swim closer calling as he did so.

"David, your coat, boy! David!!"

David, as one awakening from a sleep, immediately obeyed, taking off his cloak. Then, like his father had done before him, manipulated the garment like a rope, swinging it as close as he could to Sir John. Sir John caught the end and hung on. The coldness numbed him but he willed his energy into his wrists, his palms and his fingers. David pulled; God was gracious; one had been taken but the other had been left.

****

The people of Stallworth were unanimous in their decision to call David as pastor after the death of his father. David hemmed and hawed. Incompetency ate at him, all the more so because of the cowardice and inaction he felt he had displayed at the river's edge. Sir John's encouragement and talk of the will of God did not ease matters for him nor did the fact that Sir John himself felt responsible for the death of his father. His mother, although grieving bitterly, also urged the boy to take the place of his father, saying it would have pleased Jesse to see his child minister to the people he so loved. In the end David submitted to what he referred to as "the inclination of his duty", and agreed to serve Stallworth as its minister.

It was early in May of that same year, when Kate knocked at the door. Elizabeth, Delia, John and Althea had just sat down for supper. David was not home. John, who showed Kate in, brought her into the kitchen. Always the kind hostess, Elizabeth bad her sit in the great wooden, bee-hive chair by the chimney. It was uncommonly cold out and the wind blew with great gusts that could be felt through cracks. Elizabeth herself, once Kate was comfortably seated, sat on a chair beside her. Next to the chimney hung bacon, the rack of which covered half the ceiling. Mutton hams hung alongside. Kate eyed these as she sat, at first not saying a word. Delia looked down at the table, dark brown and shining, polished by herself that very morning. A few pewter dishes ranged along the mantelpiece shelf. And the triangular cupboard in the corner, high as the ceiling, boasted a silver saucepan, two goblets and some silver spoons. These had all been a part of Elizabeth's dowry on her marriage to Jesse and all these Kate took in. She had not said anything safe that she was Kate and that she was there to see about Delia. Because David had talked about Kate to his parents, Elizabeth was courteous to the woman, waiting to hear what she had on her mind.

Delia wore a camlet gown and a white apron. She had never been given to idle chatter, but had always been reticent. This had become even more so after Jesse's death. The girl had taken it hard. Although Elizabeth had gained Delia's confidence, it had been Jesse whom the maid had trusted with all her heart. Elizabeth saw that she was troubled at Kate's presence. Kate finally spoke.

"It's time you came back home to your mother, Delia."

The words made both Delia and Elizabeth wince. Never in all the time she had stayed at the Baxter's had Delia intimated that Kate was her mother. Elizabeth half stood up in her consternation. She wished that David was home. Delia said nothing in reply but continued to stare at the table.

"Is Kate your mother, Delia?"

Delia furtively glanced at Kate who calmly stared back at the girl with an assertive air of possession. Delia then slowly nodded at Elizabeth, but still said not a word. Elizabeth sighed. Kate turned to her and smiled.

"You thought not that I would come and take the child, did you?"

"No! No, that I did not. I did not know ...."

"Ah, then she never spoke of me?"

The words were uttered without any sentiment, but as she spoke them Kate got up and stood in front of Delia where she sat at the table. The girl blinked up at her uncertainly.

"In all that time, Delia, my poppet, you never once spoke of our life together?"

Delia shook her head and Kate smiled again.

"Well, that is strange, is it not, my love, for we have many stories between us."

Elizabeth walked over to the table and chucked Delia under the chin. Lifting up the girl's head she asked whether or not she wanted to go with her mother. Kate interposed before Delia could answer.

"Of course the child wants to go with her mother. What think you? And what does your Bible teach. 'Honor your father and your mother.' Aye, I know the Word."

There was a silence before Kate went on.

"Well, get your things together, girl. We have a long journey before us and the sooner we're away the better."

Delia stood up and went into the side room which was hers. Elizabeth faced Kate.

"How can you take her so suddenly. We've cared for ...."

"Yes, yes, I know. But that was your decision, was it not? And was it not a chance to love your neighbor as yourself?"

"David is not here to say goodbye."

"Yes, David," Kate returned, "and did he not take her from my own arms last year. And could I not have the law in here to accuse him of kidnaping?"

"He did not," Elizabeth rejoined, repeating, "He did not ...."

"It doesn't matter," Kate interrupted without letting her finish.

Retracing her steps to the door, she stood silently unresponsive to any more questions. From time to time she called out to Delia to please hurry, they had but so many hours of daylight left to travel that day. Elizabeth went into Delia's room and sat on the small bed on which the girl slept. Delia had wrapped up her clothes in a sheet and was tying it into a bundle.

"Do you want to go?"

Delia turned to her and Elizabeth was shocked to see great anger and defiance in the girl's eyes.

"Yes, and what good," the child said, "is your God? You preach mercy and love and forgiveness but then ...."

"Then what?"

"Then," said Delia, suddenly softening her voice and dropping her eyes to the floor, "then there is the remembering and I wanted to forget ... to be covered always ...."

"But," said Elizabeth, bewildered, "what do you remember? What do you want to forget? Surely, I can help. I have grown to love you, child, as my ...."

Kate's voice broke in on their words.

"Delia, don't dawdle! Come quickly now, girl!"

Delia pulled at the knot she had tied in her bundle and looked at Elizabeth.

"I am not your child," she said, " and there is no use pretending I am, for I was not born of you. And so you cannot keep me ...."

"Is she truly your mother?"

Delia's eyes filled with tears and without answering she turned and fled the room.

When David came home two days later, Kate and Delia were long gone. His mother, as well as Sir John, urged him to travel to London but the crops must be planted, the sick visited, and the sermons written. And deep within himself David, who now filled a lofty pulpit, was angry that Delia had never disclosed her parentage.

In the end it was Sir John who almost ordered David to search for the girl. He had a letter that needed to be delivered in London and he made mention of the fact that Elizabeth missed the child sorely and that it would be an act of Christian charity to look the girl up and make certain that she was provided for. David longed for Delia himself, much more than he cared to admit. Surely by this time the streets and air in London would be clean of the plague for was it not nearing the end of August. News had it that the king himself had taken up residence in Whitehall again this summer so things must be safe.

Consequently David made ready to begin another journey to London. Sir John's letter was safely tucked into his pocket, a packet of bread made ready by Althea was in his hands and a great many admonitions from his mother to bring the girl back, if at all possible, were in his heart. Before he had left, she had taken David's face between her hands and had fixedly gazed at him a long while. But she had not spoken.

David could already see London while still a day's travel away from the city. All the sky before and around it was of a fiery color, the light of which did not abate and the heat of which David could feel, the closer he came.

"Is the city burning?" he whispered to himself, "Is God so sorely vexed with her to first send the plague and then a fire."

As he came closer, he began to encounter people on the road, hundreds of them. They drove horses and pulled carts and seemed to be carrying away entire households. For the most part they were a mixture of folk, rich and poor alike. Each group had their own opinions which they freely shared with David, all of them laced with warnings to turn back. Many were of the mindset that the fire had been deliberately set by French or Dutch patriots. After all, was England not at war with both the Dutch and the French? Others were convinced that the fire heralded the Second Coming of Christ. A third opinion, mainly held by the poorer class of people traveling north, was that the Papists were out to get the Protestants and that they had begun a fire somewhere on Pudding Lane in a bakery. Queen Mary's ghost, they insisted, had opened the baker's oven, lit a fagot and then had torched all the surrounding wooden and pitch houses.

David listened and was of two minds whether to coninue on to London or not. Though he almost retraced his steps, he could not get out of his mind the picture of his father carefully making his way onto the thin ice in his attempt to rescue Sir

John. He also recalled the look his father had given him just before sinking into the blackness of the river. And so he persevered in his journey. Arriving in Moorfields, which lay just outside the city, he came across a huge contingent of homeless people. Thousands were bivouacked side by side regardless of rank, degree or age. They were, for the most part, a tired-looking company. Streaked with dirt, soot on their hands and faces, they had all been reduced to mean poverty overnight. Heaps of clothing, bedding and furniture were piled helter skelter everywhere. Tents were in the process of being erected by soldiers and the noise of talking, crying, moaning and groaning was deafening.

David stopped in the middle of the general mayhem and considered. It was not likely that he would be able to deliver Sir John's letter. Aghast at the destruction he was witnessing along the skyline, he thought of Sodom and Gomorrah. Surely it had been such a sight as he was seeing now. From where he stood it seemed as if all London was afire.

"David, David!!"

Surprised that someone would know his name, he turned and came face to face with Robert Heath.

"David, how come you here?"

"I came to deliver a letter."

In spite of the horrible situation, both of them laughed, albeit not long. Robert was covered with soot, his hands were blistered and his shoes were in tatters.

"Each time you come it seems London has some disastrous belly-ache."

"How... How is your family?"

David was not sure he ought to ask, as he surmised that very likely Robert's wife and children had died.

"My wife is over yonder. I have settled her in a tent of sorts. And we have one child left."

He stopped short and turned to face the city before he continued.

"Well, are you staying? Or will you turn and head homewards again?"

"I've also come to find out whether Delia, Kate's daughter, whether she is well ....?"

He ended on a questioning note. Robert's voice, as he answered, registered surprise.

"Kate's daughter?"

Then he repeated the words again, as if to himself.

"Kate's daughter?"

"Yes, you know the child she was speaking of last time I was here. The child I took home with me and who lived with my parents for a season. A few months ago, Kate arrived in Stallworth to take Delia back to London to live with her again."

Robert looked at him strangely.

"So you want to find Delia?"

"Yes, my mother was most fond of her and I ...."

He stopped. What indeed did he really think of Delia? Delia, the naked child whom he had taken from the window; Delia, the girl whom he had led to his home; Delia, the girl whom his father had taught. His thoughts were interrupted by Robert.

"She is not Kate's daughter, you know."

"She is not Kate's daughter?"

He said the words after Robert, not understanding.

"No, she is not. Indeed, Kate is as far from a mother as you can find throughout all London. She ran a brothel on Throckmorton Street and lately, after the plague abated, moved her 'shop' more to the south."

"Then Delia ...?"

David stopped, horrified and disgusted. That was why the girl had never spoken of her past.

"Yes, the girl was one of the ... one of the wares, you might say, with which Kate plied her trade. They say even the king visited her establishment."

David turned away.

"You will not be wanting to see her then?"

"No!"

David spat the word out but from the past, above the din of the people, he clearly heard Delia's voice.

"We'd a parson down the street from us. He was the first one to leave. Preached about the wrath of God and then left. It's always the poor ones who receive the wrath and it's always the rich ones who run away from it."

Robert's voice returned him to the present.

"I have seen the whole south of London burning from Cheapeside to the Thames and all along Cornehill, Tower Street, Fenchurch Street, Gracious Street and up to Bainard's Castle. They hope that St. Paul's, as it is made of brick, will stand safe. The streets are all chaos. Miles and miles are strewn with moveables of all sorts and the sky is like a burning oven above. The cracking and thunder of the flames, the shrieking of the men and women and children is awful. The air is so hot it engulfs you. It's not likely in any case, you see, that either Kate or Delia, or any of her girls are still alive. The burning continues."

David nodded. He was suddenly extremely weary even though, by all the standards around him, he was clean, well-fed and not in any dire straits.

"Come over and meet my wife. She's been wanting to thank you for the money."

Fanny Heath was a pretty woman. Small-boned, with deep, blue eyes, she shone with contentment. David could not fathom it when he first looked at her. Here was a woman who had lost four children as well as her home but she was still smiling - and smiling with such warmth and peacefulness.

"Welcome," she said.

There was nothing really that she was welcoming him to. There was but a bit of tarp, from off Robert's boat, no doubt, set up so that there was a shelter of sorts. A table, and three chairs, probably salvaged from their small house by the Thames, as well as some bedding was all that stood on the small rectangular piece of Moorfields she had made her own. The little girl whom he had seen with her before, clung to her skirts.

"This is Mary," she said and the child hid her face but not before she had dimpled at David, and Fanny added, "You must be hungry?"

"No, no, you mustn't trouble yourself. I've eaten."

Fanny persisted.

"The king has freely sent much bread and cheese out here from the Navy Stores. So I can offer you food."

Still David shook his head. She continued.

"Robert has said that you are a pastor. Might I ask you to pray with me and a small group of people who are also of a mind to ask God to keep us safe?"

David nodded. What else could he do but agree.

After Fanny had left to collect her friends, David felt his heart so dry and unaffected by her request that he knew he would not be able to pray. He could not, for all the burning and misery around him, feel anything close to a desire to speak with God. There was only an intense anger. Moving away from the place where the Heaths had set up, he saw that Robert had begun walking towards London. Running after the man, he caught up saying that he had changed his mind, and that he would, after all, like to find both Kate and Delia. Robert looked somewhat surprised but only acknowledged the information with a quick inclination of his head while he kept walking. David tagged along.

"Where are you going?" David asked presently, as Robert followed a somewhat westerly path into the city.

Robert did not answer. There was tremendous disorder everywhere. Many people, fleeing without apparent direction, ran through the streets. There was much shouting and crying. As they passed one half-burned building, they saw a kitten being taken out of a hole in a chimney with the hair all burned off its body. Yet its mewling indicated life.

"And even though the kitten lives," David said presently, "how shall the poor thing survive? Naked as it was born and twice as susceptible."

"We none of us can live without help," Robert answered and kept on walking.

David felt chastised but knew not why. Amid all the destruction he'd had no time to think and that is what he wanted. His thoughts, pushed down within himself, were accusing him and he liked them not. In due time David found himself by the west walls on Ludgate close to St. Paul's. The majestic church, completely built of stone, stood alone. All the houses around it had burned down. Strangely enough, even as David and Robert craned their necks scanning the edifice, the great building took fire. It was not at the ground level, where it would have been expected, but at the very top. The lead in the steeple visibly trickled down. A few poor and besmirched pigeons, loath to fly away from the roof they called home, hovered about the spires until they burned their wings and began a downward descent. Even though it was by now full evening, London's fire was so conspicuous that it seemed as if night had been swallowed up in its blaze.

"I know where Delia might be, if she be yet alive."

Robert suddenly spoke and turned to face David.

"Where?"

David, the light of the flames playing on his face, answered quickly, too quickly, exposing his heart. Robert did not answer, but walked away from St. Paul's, setting out in the direction of Whitehall. Many of the houses there, as well as surrounding buildings, were being destroyed to create open spaces across which the sparks could not jump.

"Where?"

David repeated the question as he followed Robert. The noise of beams falling and stone masonry collapsing with great crash and clatter, faded behind them.

"Kate knows my brother and my brother has told me that she moved from Throckmorton to a house just a little further. You will see it soon enough."

Through the billowing clouds of smoke the moon could be seen every now and then. It was a strange sight - a pale moon over a red landscape. They stopped in front of a three-storied home. Here too, as in other parts of the city, people milled about on the street, scrutinizing the sky for signs as to whether or not they should begin to save their goods.

"You must knock here," Robert told David.

"But what shall I ...? Who lives here and ...?

Robert merely looked at him as David spoke and did not reply to his stuttering inquiries. Then, lifting his hand in a gesture of farewell, he turned back and disappeared into the crowd. David watched him go and then appraised the house. He recalled with clarity how he had stood by another house and how he had received Delia into his arms. Only for a moment he had held her and then he had put her down on the ground. He recalled also that he'd had pity on her, so beautiful she had seemed to him, so vulnerable in her nakedness.

"Eh, sir, what do you think," an old man accosted him, "should I take my cloak with me or not?"

He did not respond and left the old man standing in the middle of his unanswered question, as he resolutely approached the door and knocked. There was no answer. He knocked again and again before he commenced to pounding. At that point Kate opened the door.

"Well," she said, and that was all she said.

She stood as he remembered her in the window, hands on her hips, imperious and somewhat dark, the black, impudent waistcoat bodice the same.

"I've come for Delia."

"Have you."

It was not a question but a negative answer.

"Yes, I'd like to see her."

This made Kate laugh.

"Well, sir, it will cost you to see her, and not a little either."

David was shocked although he kept his face inscrutable.

"How much."

"Five shillings."

The doddering, old man, who had touched him before, tapped his shoulder again.

"What do you think sir," he repeated, somewhat addled, "should I take my cloak then? Is it necessary do you think, or not?"

David smiled and answered him this time.

"Yes, I think you should never go anywhere without it."

The man was satisfied and walked away. Kate had stepped outside. She had a scowl on her face and eyed the bright redness of the sky somewhat uneasily. Taking advantage of her distraction, David moved into the dingy hall.

"You must pay me first."

She followed close at his heels.

"I must see Delia and if you don't show me where she is, I'll find her myself."

He strode on, straight up a stairs in front of him. Kate was at his tail, trying to impede his progress by pulling at his breeches. But he took the steps two at a time, shaking her off. At the top of the flight he had the choice of either going down a hallway, or going up yet another stairs. He chose the stairs, almost flying up. At the very top there was a door. Reaching it, he flung it open. The room held a dresser and a bed but nothing else. Doing an about-face he ran down again. Kate stood in the hallway, guarding access to a drab and seedy-looking door.

"You must let me in."

She smirked and opened wide for him. David saw a bed covered with a grimy blanket. There was a form under the bedcover, a form hunched up in a fetal position. He froze. Kate chortled in triumph over his discomfort and, ambling over to the bed, in one fell motion whipped the covers off the form. Exposed and shamed, Delia lay on the mattress, naked and defenseless. She did not look up but tried to cover herself with her arms. Kate faced David, spittle running down her chin in her eagerness to speak.

"Here's your fine madam, lad. Take her if you like. No use to me, she is, four months in the family way with manners too high and mighty for this place."

Leaning against the bed railing, she continued.

"But you don't want her, do you, parson!! You only like the good and the pure and the holy." She retreated back into the semi-darkness of the hall, fully expecting David to follow her there. But infinitely moved beyond himself, David undid the cloak on his back and gently covered Delia with the corner of his garment.

Glossary

Batzen - silver coin

Beguine - member of a Christian sisterhood founded in the 12th century. Although not taking religious vows, a beguine followed an austere life

Burgermeister - mayor

Burse - a flat, square case in which communion bread is carried by Roman Catholic priests

Camlet - fabric made of silk and wool or goat's hair

Chimere - a loose, sleeveless robe worn by bishops

Chuff-headed - conceited, pleased with one-self

Cudgel - short, thick stick used as a weapon

Dominican - member of an order of friars founded in 1215 dedicated especially to preaching

Ein feste Burg - a might fortress (hymn by Luther and sung by many Protestants)

Ferule - long-handled spoon

Fichu - small triangular shawl, worn around a woman's shoulders and neck

Fenestral window - casement window attached to its frame by one or more hinges

Franciscan - monk of the order founded in 1209 by Francis of Assisi

Gabardine - ankle-length loose coat of spun fabric

Genuflect - bend one knee to the ground, as in worship

Lehrmeister - teacher

Major-domo - chief steward of a large household

Matins - morning prayers

Meisterin - mistress

Monolith - large building or structure

Pantoffles - slippers

Pleached - intertwined, interlaced (tree branches) to form a hedge

Pollarded - trimmed, pruned

Pravity - wickedness, depravity

Prioress - head of a house of certain orders of nuns, ranked below abbess

Pyx - small round metal receptacle in which communion bread is kept by Roman Catholic priests

Refectory - room used for communal meals in an educational or religious institution

Rochet - white linen vestment worn by bishops

Runagate - vagabond

Wherry - light rowboat